Romancing the Buzzard

Romancing the Buzzard

Leah Murray

QUATTRO BOOKS

The publication of *Romancing the Buzzard* has been generously supported by the Canada Council for the Arts and the Ontario Arts Council.

Cover design: Diane Mascherin
Cover image: Leah Murray
Author's photo: Leah Murray
Typography: Grey Wolf Typography
Editor: Luciano Iacobelli

Murray, Leah
      Romancing the buzzard / Leah Murray.

Issued also in electronic format.
ISBN 978-1-926802-92-3

      1. Rosato, Tony--Fiction. 2. Murray, Leah, 1956- --Fiction. I. Title.

PS8626.U7765R65 2012   C813'.6   C2012-900345-X

Published by Quattro Books Inc.
89 Pinewood Avenue
Toronto, Ontario, M6C 2V2
www.quattrobooks.ca

Printed in Canada

For Ben and Nathaniel.

For my secret supernova.

One

the call to adventure: frog

1.
unflinching

my amphibious
skin glistens, blisters, as once
tepid water boils

2.
still smelling of warm round gold

my newly bereft
hands wait for a frog, the width
and breadth of my tongue

Soft summer night, I lie in bed, overcome by thrills, touching my nine-year old buds of breasts, and heaving nine-hundred-year old sighs at the open window. Sleepless hours that kiss pillows, tug blankets, stroke and dust my cheeks with tears. Full round drops that slide from my eyes and trace the folds of my ears with the smoothness of bears. I pretend I am driving my body like a speeding car, my skin, a rain-speckled windshield, aware of every droplet's zigzagging lifespan, every slanted water snake inching its way up my humming engine spine, and across my translucent forehead.

And when I close my eyes, I am spinning to the left, dervish dancing, whirling on my axis, that imaginary line about which my body rotates, my skirt billowing out, like a shroud and like the sky, my right hand lifted, palm-out, my head tilted to the left, always to the left, always like blood circulating around the heart, like pivoting planets, counter-clockwise. And I swear I can feel what the earth must feel, sublime velocity, dazzling arcs of momentum, as it and I hurtle through space. But like a spinning coin, I suddenly fall to one side with a shudder, then a twirling sound, then a rattle of surging speed until I stop abruptly, heart-stoppingly still, suspended delicately, hung between the breezeless stars.

It goes like this all night, night after night. My body throbs and buzzes like power lines, expanding and contracting with the galaxies and the chambers of my heart, my head as big as the universe and as tiny as a small grey pencil dot. And my heart is a pendulum, oscillating with each heartbeat, the curved line that connects all staccato spots of light, or drops of blood, the satin string that sews each wobbling star to all the others, and me to him.

Because that is who I am waiting for. I do not know who he is, and I am not old enough yet, but soon, soon. My pendulum is also a dowser, divining the answer to all yes/no questions, predicting with an accuracy as certain as the pinpoint cosmos was, in the instant it exploded its dense milky matter outward, that it would surely one day collapse back in on itself, a crumbling cage of dinosaur bones suddenly fainting into a cloud of sparkly chalk.

Already fixed in the stars, in the light entering my eyes just now but from a million years long gone, is my orbit and who I circle around, my course and his course, x and y axes, their intersection unavoidable. Looking dizzy up into the night sky, or into the black-red undersides of my eyelids, it is the same as looking back in time. I see how my own private constellation has been mapped out, how it propels me into the future.

I see my own infant heart here, too. I feel it like a captive wild bird, blind and fluttering fiercely against its bone aviary, ceaseless, despite never cracking into daylight, despite never a hint that escape is even an option. I put my fingers in my ears and listen to the chirping, to the pumping of wings, hear my blood echo and roar like a hot ocean, its waves sent travelling by electrical signals, pulsating with the same primordial lightning that quickened me out of the slime.

Eventually, I am able to soothe my small red cardinal, broken feathered, his startled black eyes blinking. I count steady lungfuls of breath, rhythmically inspiring and expiring, letting the air breathe *me*. I imagine I am a knotted, wrinkled bed sheet, slowly being loosened and spread open into a giant garment press, and then squeezed tightly in the hugest of hugs, uncreased, immaculate. And I am as white and blank as the faces of five British monks, in the summer of 1178, witnessing an asteroid crash into the upper of the moon's two horns, which splits apart and spews fire. And though it goes against all their religious certainties, they see the moon swinging like a bell.

And then he comes to me in my girlhood sleep, my tender kind murderer, my bad saint. My giver of solace, my inflictor of despair. My albatross, my vulture. The one who fills and then empties, the one who adores and then does not. The one who levels me, pins me down and sweats into my eyes, the one who razes me to the ground, remorseless, my Tunguska fireball, because, he "has to," he says. He "has no choice." This is the only way for me, his new green shoot, to nudge my head up through the dark dirt into the approval of his shining sun face. My guilty protector and my innocent offender. My lover and my assailant. My husband, my executioner.

Often, he bursts into my dreams like a god through a cleft in the earth where I am picking flowers, ready to trick me with a handful of pomegranate seeds. Sometimes, I am a thousand flies and he is a chimney swift, spending his entire life in the air, catching and eating me. Or I am a leaf, and he is a tired tent bat, biting through my ribs to make me droop down and cover him during the night. But mostly, we are both frogs, and he climbs onto my back and hides eggs between my shoulder blades. There, in small pits, something hatches.

Two

MARCH 8, 2006

Attention: Ms. Priscilla Christie, Crown Attorney

Dear Ms. Christie,

Ms. Murray has been severely traumatized from her experiences with her husband. She is recovering from Post Traumatic Stress Disorder, and seeing this man will worsen her symptoms. For the purposes of testifying in court, it would be preferable, for medical reasons, if she could testify on closed circuit television or with a screen between her and the defendant so as to avoid triggering her symptoms.

Sincerely,

Joe Burley M.D.

March 15, 2006

HER MAJESTY THE QUEEN V. ANTONIO ROSATO

CHARGE: Criminal Harassment

PRELIMINARY INQUIRY

APPEARANCES

Ms. P. Christie – Counsel for the Crown

Ms. F. Hawthorn – Counsel for the Accused

CROSS-EXAMINATION BY MS. HAWTHORN

MS. HAWTHORN: So I understand when December rolled around, somebody thought it would be nice to get married on New Year's Eve.

LEAH MURRAY: Yes.

Q. And whose idea was that?

A. It was both our idea. He kept saying over and over again, "You're never going to marry me, are you? You don't really love me. If you really loved me you would agree to marry me right now."
And so I said, "Okay, let's get married. Let's get married on December 31."

Q. And did you go out and make the arrangements for that?

A. Yes, we went that morning to Kingston City Hall to get the license, and then we went on the bus to Toronto City Hall to have the actual ceremony.

Q. And this was a mutually agreed-upon thing.

A. Yes.

Bloodstain pattern analysts may be able to determine the movement and direction of a person while he or she was shedding blood, the origin of an impact pattern, the number of impacts during an incident, and the sequence of events.

He proposes marriage to me three times. The first proposal comes in October, on our second date. I'm sitting on his lap in a private karaoke room, and he just says it. "Let's get married." I laugh and say yes.

The second is a month later in my kitchen. We've just finished doing the dishes. He gets down on one knee and holds both my hands in his still damp ones. He says earnest and heartfelt words, and then asks me formally. I smile and say yes.

The third is a few weeks after that, at the 2003 Canadian Aboriginal Music Awards. We have just come from the Eaton Centre, where I'd watched him, his forehead slick with sweat, draw four hundred dollars from the cash machine to pay for my engagement ring. It's platinum, with a large blue topaz. I don't even like it, but he's convinced that I do. I go along with it because he seems so pleased with his choice, and I don't want to hurt his feelings.

And so we're sitting in movie theatre seats, awkwardly waiting for the ceremonies to start, crowded on all sides by turquoise-bedecked Native ladies. He gives me the blue topaz ring right then and there in a blue felt heart-shaped box. He takes the ring out of the box, and asks me to marry him. I say yes, and he slips the ring onto the fourth finger of my right hand. Then, almost as an afterthought, he pulls out an identical second blue felt heart-shaped box and says he just can't wait to give me my actual wedding band, and here it is, and could I wear it also? I feel my throat tighten as Native lady ears and eyes hum close around us like fireflies in the now darkening, hushed room. "Okay," I say, and he squeezes the wedding band onto my left hand ring finger. "A bit tight," I say, and he is crestfallen and slightly annoyed, as though my finger is too big on purpose. He looks away.

"Here," he says, and plunks both empty ring boxes in my lap. "These are beautiful. You should keep them." I put them in my coat pocket.

Projected bloodstains occur when some form of energy has been transferred, and causes drops to form in elliptical shapes. Medium velocity impact spatters are typically the result of beatings, and high velocity impact patterns appear as a mist-like spray of droplets, the result of gunshots or explosions.

In December, he decides that I'll wear the blue topaz engagement ring only on very special occasions, but that I should wear my wedding band at all times, except whenever I have to clean the kitty litter – he thinks it's disrespectful otherwise. So I comply. Every time I perform this chore, I remove my ring and put it carefully back into its heart-shaped box, which I keep on my dresser. The other heart-shaped box with my blue topaz engagement ring inside it is in my sock drawer for safekeeping. But one day, as I reach for something on my dresser, I knock the wedding band ring box to the floor, and it breaks in two, the hinges snapping apart.

Passive bloodstains are those created by the force of gravity. Free-falling blood has low velocity, and leaves large round drops, as found in the case of suicides.

My first thought is that he is going to be very disturbed by this. He'll assume my carelessness with his gift to me reveals a lack of love for him. So I hide the broken ring box. I put it in an old shoebox filled with old photos and things I never look at, and I shove it into the furthest, darkest corner of my closet. Then I put another box of old junk on top of that one, just in case. Then I find an old regular square-shaped jewellery store box, put my blue topaz engagement ring in that one, and stick it back in my sock drawer, so I can use the unbroken heart-shaped box for my wedding band, and keep it on top of my dresser like usual, so he won't know what I've done.

Forensic investigators look at crime scenes and give expert scientific opinions to families who desperately want to focus

their blame and anger, their sadness. Was their loved one the victim of a murder? Or was it suicide?

After a week, the incident slips from the forefront of my mind. Until one day, I come home and notice the heart-shaped box on top of my dresser is broken. I ask him if he knows what happened to it. He looks at me, bemused. "I have no idea, darling," he says. I go back to my bedroom with a sick, sick hunch in my gut. My stomach feels like a clammy, clenched fist as I venture into my closet, looking for that old shoebox. Everything is just how I left it, with the second box of old junk on top. But I dig it out anyway. And I find it. The unbroken heart-shaped box, in the exact spot I buried the broken one.

And sometimes, despite the evidence, families refuse to believe. "What do you mean?" they ask. "She would never kill herself! We would have known if something was wrong. No, she was smart. She would have come to us for help."

And so I sit in that black hole corner of my closet for a long time, wondering what to do. My heart slows to a dull, dawdling thud, the blood in my arteries feels cold and congealed, but it gets pulled earthward by the tug of gravity into my feet, where it pools in large round drops, before my veins remind themselves to look up, to take the blood on that familiar journey to the heart.

Sometimes families have reason to wonder, because evidence isn't always conclusive, a finding can be just an investigator's best guess. And no one can ever really know what happened, or why, sometimes not even the people who were there.

After a while I get out of my closet. I stand up. I brush myself off. And then I go ask him what we're doing for dinner.

him, preparing meals for me

he makes sandwiches
with peanut butter and jam
and honey   this for more sweetness

he cooks spaghetti sauce
with whole cloves of roasted garlic
like this   is all that matters

and then there are chicken legs
dripping in hot sauce
entire lives leading   to just this

my favourite is salad
I love to watch him
pouring the oil and vinegar
he mixes these with the lettuce
without utensils
only his hands
I will think about this   with each bite

Three

She has a rock.

A piece of slate, the most common neighbourhood kind, a fine-grained, homogenous, metamorphic rock, passing what feels like unbearably huge packages of time that also seem to blink by, sitting on her window sill, stacking dust particles, witnessing her own random, insoluble comings and goings. Her moods, with no discernible patterns, her wants, her chagrins, her sleeps and wakes, her purposes amounting to nothing greater than what kind of gum she chews or how many pieces, how many bubbles she can blow, and how big she can make them. And all of a sudden, more time passing, the gum getting hard, her heart soft, knees weak, the days harsh, her eyes wet, genitals dry, and wondering, when was the last time she ate? Where is her new doctor's office? What bills does she need to pay? What kind of life is this? This life of non-negotiable chores and errands, of everything she hates, just to stay living.

She has a plant.

A peace lily, Spathiphyllum, evergreen perennial, cleaning the air for her, unasked, not needing excessive moisture and light to survive, as mildly toxic as possible when ingested, as though a favour to her or fellow living creatures. But no longer growing its white bloom with its yellow spathe, no longer predictably requiring care, or so it seems, going weeks without needing to be watered, standing straight up, leaves and stems turgid, proud, making her think, *Perhaps I will wait until tomorrow to water it.* And then tomorrow comes, and she wakes up, does not notice it at first, but then later, catches it in her peripheral vision – a small quake of heartache, split-second of surprise gushing through her own cells – she sees it sprawling downwards, leaves of wilted crêpe paper, stems like limp, dishevelled hair or empty socks. And for the entire rest of the night and into the next morning, she replays the scene in her brain like a record player stuck in a loop, the realization that she has again waited too long, stunning her like blanket fog or asphyxia.

She has a body.

A sea sponge, phylum Porifera, sessile and aquatic, having no nervous, digestive or circulatory system, then moving on to a starfish, class Asteroidea, an opportunistic feeder, but losing all five arms and the ability to regenerate, then again moving on, this time to her own, chordate mammal, the full catastrophe, proving most difficult of all. Finally peeling back the veneer and the integument to reveal the side of the opening, the in-between: she sees some girl in a ceaseless, shapeless panic over the human condition with no option of pacifying it or evading it or shaking it off. From the first moment of waking to the moment of waking again, it is there, this dull, pounding smothering, so relentless, thinking of dying becomes not a weighty, emotional dilemma, but a sweet, diaphanous daydream of relief. Because there is no distraction or escape other than death, no clawing out of rubble in an earthquake, no swimming to the surface after a capsize, no finding shelter during a tornado. This is being never freed from the trap of the present moment, like never pushing aside that final sunlight-blocking brick, never getting that rapturous, lung-aching gasp of air, never fleeing the frenzied, jagged wind, because there never was a before and then an after, a confinement and then a release, pain and then freedom from pain. There is only ever this, now.

She has a soul.

A metaphysical sense of identity, formerly clinging to a mother, who, looking right through her, always unsmiling, reminding her often, that even as a baby, "You didn't like to be touched," and a father, never affectionate or available, never saying things like, "I love you, honey, I'll protect you from that wild world," and now to someone else: this man.

This man, the same age as her father, who, coming in and walking straight up, folds her into him like he would never let her go, and says, "I love you, honey, I'll protect you from that wild world," making her want to follow him forever, to rub her face into his neck and his bedclothes, to breathe him in, in, in, so craving him, wanting even the dust from his shoes on her shoes.

And longing to forget herself and her dread-stricken life, she climbs into him and feels relief for the first time, asking him again and again, "Is this the way?"

And again and again he answers, "Yes, my darling, your eyes and your lips and your tongue are the stairs, your doubt and your lack of doubt, your giving up and your persevering, put it all under your feet, and use it to climb higher into me, further into the safety of my arms."

March 15, 2006

HER MAJESTY THE QUEEN V. ANTONIO ROSATO

CHARGE: Criminal Harassment

PRELIMINARY INQUIRY continued.

<u>CROSS-EXAMINATION BY MS. HAWTHORN continued.</u>

MS. HAWTHORN: So did you not consider leaving Tony when the bad very much outweighed the good?

LEAH MURRAY: I didn't think I had a choice, because by that point I was pregnant, and we were married, and he had said to me over and over and over again that we were married in the Catholic Church so our sacrament could not be broken, and that's just the way it was. I didn't know there were options out there, that there was a way to get help. I really thought, This is it – this is my situation in life, and this is what I have to deal with.

Q. But you had a mom. You didn't phone her?

A. No, I didn't confide in her.

Q. And you had a dad.

A. Yes, I was too scared. I was very, very intimidated by Tony. I was just so afraid to do anything wrong or say anything wrong, and he told me again and again that a wife is never supposed to say anything bad about her husband. I couldn't even bring myself to talk about it anonymously with the priest in confession. He had this power over me, and I was completely submissive. I couldn't stand up for myself. I was absolutely mind-controlled.

Q. So you didn't talk to your mom, you didn't talk to your dad, you didn't talk to your brothers.

A. I was too afraid he would somehow find out I had been talking badly about him behind his back.

Q. You say you fell in love with him, that he had wonderful features, but wouldn't you agree with me that at a certain point you would fall out of love with him? Like, he would do bad things, and you'd think, well, maybe he's not such a kind, tender person after all.

A. I think somebody on the outside looking in would say that, but when you're actually in that relationship, and you've invested already so much into that person, it clouds things for you. I fell in love with him so deeply I wanted to look past all the bad things. The times when he was kind and gentle and funny, and the times when he took care of me…that's who I wanted. That's who I thought he could be.

Q. So you were deeply in love with these wonderful characteristics he had.

A. Yes.

Q. And the bad characteristics didn't detract from the depth of love of the good characteristics?

A. I overlooked them at first. When they weren't really, really bad, I overlooked them.

Q. Well, you actually overlooked them for over a year. Because you started noticing these negative characteristics you've told us about before you ever got married to him, although you say they were milder then, and you say they got worse over time.

A. Yes, I overlooked them from the beginning, that's true, yes, but I didn't overlook them all the way through the whole relationship, because they were ultimately what caused me to leave him.

Q. There must have come a point early on where you thought to yourself: this relationship is going nowhere. Didn't you reach that point?

A. Yes, but I can't express how much he controlled me, and how much of an emotionally low place I had come to because of that. I had no self-esteem, I had no confidence, I had no ability to stand up for myself. I knew he was being abusive to me, and I knew it was wrong, but I did not have the ability to leave him then. I was overcome with fear. I was overcome with the feeling that there was nothing I could do.

Night air   thick
wading into heat
oh god oh god oh god help me
there's nowhere to run
bootstep echoes come
pulsing up the stairs
like sonar   sussing me
damp haired
sweat trickling
my neck   eel slick
maybe when the baby's born
he'll be good he'll be good

but later   hiding
outside with baby
between cold pillars of streetlight
oh god oh god oh god help me
snow comes soft purr
sea foam breath
my ears   thick quiet
gentle updraft   and
for a moment
snow falls skyward
upside down star spouts
he's worse he's worse

Four

Here is a man. Full grown, Mediterranean-blooded, the kind of man who could walk straight up to her, look her over and say, "Come here," and she would come. Only he doesn't do that. Not right away. Their first conversation ends with him, plaintive, supplicant-faced, asking her to stay in his life. He fastens her eyes with his, and puts his palms together, fingers interlocked, and she feels his plea rumble under her skin, and contract through her muscles with a sound like thunder that quivers her, unswerving, down past bone and into marrow. Earthworms abandon their winter burrows. Goldfish jump out of their water. Catfish thrash. She cannot say no.

And then comes the lure of the primitive in him, the landslide of longing for his large, rough hands on her thighs. He can turn to her at any time and lift up her chin with the tips of his fingers, bringing her mouth to meet his. He can sink to his knees and slowly untie her boots without asking.

And when he leads her to the bedroom, it is like entering another world, not congruent with anything else she has experienced before. He kisses her for hours, until she is not just a small dot of awareness in a body, but a glowing planet of consciousness, where her knees and belly and neck and eyelids are continents bathed in moonlight.

She remembers a story about a man who wanted to learn how to use a palette knife but could not find any books to teach him. So the man decided to take the knife in his hand like he was the first to ever hold one, the first to ever mix pigment or apply paint to canvas with a flexible steel blade.

He makes her feel as though *she* is *his* palette knife, an extension of his wrist, his arm, his soul even, so essential to whatever it is they were creating, some gorgeous and lush alchemy of brow sweat and mingled dyes, of blood and vibrant-coloured minerals and precious stones, hand-crushed and burned.

She stops wanting to hear her own name, because whenever he speaks it, it is at the exclusion of all the other beautiful names he uses for her – baby, honey, sweetheart. All his words sound like poetry, make the humdrum of day-to-day life peel away like sheets of old wallpaper. "I love your all," he says to her, "your smiles, your laughs, your tears, the way you shake your hips when you sing Elvis, the way you walk around in your long johns, the curve of your lips, the lilt of your vibrato, the gentle struggle of your hand finding its way to holding my arm. You are sunlight on my face on my happiest day, my most comfortable sleep when I am not sure if I am a babe or a man or both, my most beautiful secret, soft in your arms like arriving home and living there always, curled up in that blanket of joy. You are like stepping into a magical valley where I would forever set up camp, sipping from a stream that washes my lonely throat with soft truths of you." He comes into her life offering things she never even knew she wanted from another human being until now. So many promises of adventure, promises to take care of her and protect her, promises to love and adore her even past death or the end of the world. He says he will sweep away all her loneliness, and he does. He makes it so easy to say yes, to get caught under the wheels of his runaway spell, to not pull away from his compelling, ardent eyes. And so powerful his eyes are, so carefully fixed on her, that any distance is meaningless. He is often away for work, but even when he is not there, he is there.

I will always stand in the rain with you, he writes to her,
I will always stand in the sun with you
i will always stand with you
i will always with you
i will always you
i always you (as I lose my will)
i you
iyou

I reach for you
with a thousand hands
and my eyes closed

  even fish have no eyes at these depths

and the cold brings me closer to you

  I am memorizing your skin by feel

never wanting to know what it is
to miss you
miss the weight of you
ponderous, pressed into my shoulder

and when I dream, I have not arms
but thick rope
my palms, lassoes

  I am wild at these depths
  forgive me

I love you so much
I cannot sleep

Five

Now this is where Tony's defence lawyer, Ms. Hawthorn, comes a little bit unstuck with my story.

"Because, first of all," she says, "He doesn't want you to see your male friends, then he doesn't want you to see your female friends, your parents don't like him, and yet within four months you get married to him. Why don't you just say, this guy's a weirdo, I'm just going to back away from this relationship? Because you know right from the beginning, if your evidence is true. Why don't you just back away?"

"I am in love with him."

I am in love with him.

And all over the universe there are cosmic catastrophes. Galaxies are colliding, stars are exploding, like his heart and my heart are colliding and exploding. These interstellar fireworks, where in the beginning never was so much joy in so much tumult, now fly apart with a more sinister detonation, and illuminate in him the battle between two mysterious and invisible forces – one that keeps us together, and one that tears us apart – and my own struggle to understand these forces and see beyond the darkness in him.

Because I am already all in, Ms. Hawthorn. That's why I don't just back away. In the beginning, kindness is all he shows me, and anything he asks me to do I will do. Anything he wants me to give up I will give up, and it *has* been like a death of my former self, but we see it as the birth of a new me, a better me, a me that is more suited for a man like him.

So I do away with all the things he doesn't like about me, bad habits, things I don't like about myself, and some nice things, some of my favourite things, too. So enough of runny eggs on a plate, damp grass, and dull teeth, close places with strangers, my hair, ruled by humidity, twisting and curling after it rains, my lucky lighter, seasickness, and sounds, like fridge buzz, hotel neon hum, and echoes in the subway station, and music, half-remembered, aching, sweet, fond, and wavering, rusted, rough, surprised. And enough Vaseline on the lens, vitamins, and black mascara, my soft spot for birds, wind through trees like an arrow, blur-edged and supple with sky, traffic lights, and various stages of undress, and touch from any other, like handshakes, nape-neck kisses, or smooth expanses of skin on skin, or fingers, strong, purposed, tracing, mapping veins like explorers naming tributaries.

But it's not enough. I haven't done enough to make him happy, and now he is angry and mean and it's my fault, he says. And it goes like this, again and again, except he gets worse over time, like the phantom energy that expands and dilutes the cosmos, that tears up the solar systems, and then the stars, and then rips apart even my atoms, until I am nothing more than a layer of foam floating on a vast sea of his ever broadening darkness.

Then, like faint light through fog, he apologizes, and he becomes the invisible halo that cradles all the galaxies, the scaffolding ordinary matter lives inside, the skeleton that allows the universe as I know it, the trillions of stars and planets, and life and love, to hold together. And I remember, Ms. Hawthorn, why I don't just back away. He promises never to treat me badly again, and I believe him, and I forgive him.

And every time I think he won't do it again.

And every time he does.

And then I realize I am in too deep, the haze is too thick, I cannot see beyond the darkness because he is teeming with it. And now it's in me, and in the shadows, in the corner of my own bedroom, and in the deepest fathoms of space.

Three Apologies

1.
I am so sorry,
darling,
please unlock the door
and come out from the bathroom.
I miss you.
From now on,
I promise to be good.

2.
Forgive me,
my sweetest angel,
I was out of line.
But it was only because I love you so much!
And you make me die a little
when you look at other men.
(I would never hurt *your* feelings like that.)
Please stop crying.
I promise to never get angry again.
Please just love me
and honour me
enough to not upset me
again.

3.
Oh! A thousand apologies,
my dearest heart,
I hate myself for what I've done to you.
I am just a wretched man,
and your love is the only thing that can save me.
I beg you,
on my hands and knees,
don't leave me.

Do you want to be responsible for killing me?
Because I will die without you.
And frankly,
I don't think you can make it without me either.
I am worried about your sanity,
kiddo,
and if you ever dare
antagonize me like that again,
I'll have to assume you're not in your right mind and I'll be
forced to commit you to the psychiatric ward and when our
baby is born I'll have them take her away from you because any
wife who treats her husband so repulsively is an unfit mother
and no one will ever believe you if you deny it, I'll see to that.
So dry those tears,
my good little soldier.
I do these things
to help you,
to make you a better person.
And anyway,
no one but me
could ever love you.

Six

One summer night, as we walk hand-in-hand through the overgrown grass of the school grounds beside my apartment building, I tell him I have never seen a shooting star before. "You will," he says, and we gaze up at the night sky together, two tiny specks of dust staring into an infinity of frozen bees. *How unchanging*, I think, *how huge and cold, this cement ceiling of sky, pinning us like ants to the earth.*

But as we stand there, he puts his arm around me, and I tuck into his warmth, feel it seep into my skin, my blood, my mitochondria, and suddenly I feel less crushed by the night, and more enveloped into its softness. And the bees wobble, they blink on and off, and I see one of them move. One of them thaws and comes to life and streaks bright hot yellow across the blue-black velvet sky. "I told you," he says, his face as wide and smiling as the sun.

It is so easy to believe in him. When he tells me he can feel energies and communicate on a cosmic level with all living things, I think, *Who am I to judge? Who am I to know what's possible and what isn't? Who am I to tell this man, who has been so right about so many things, that he is completely wrong about this one?* And it doesn't make me love him any less. In fact, it only heightens his appeal, this mysterious, mystical quality in him that I long to understand.

Our relationship establishes itself very early on with him at the helm, and me as his underling, expected to follow his rules and trust his sense of direction. He is like the earth, and I, the moon – a magnet subject to his gravitational whims. Certainly, I have some effect on him, like the lunar tides: the moon is strong enough to pull water from the earth, and the earth lets it, both bodies grasping for closeness. But I, being smaller, always bend my path to suit his.

So I make the leap with him when he tells me he is communicating with angels. I am vaguely uneasy, but the messages he receives are so beautiful, so full of love and sweetness and poetry, it is difficult to see the harm.

He is an artist, the eccentric kind. This is how he interprets emotion, expresses his creativity. I tell myself he is a spiritual Renaissance man, like William Blake, whom I adore, who had visions and saw God put His head to the window.

*

He is in the habit of rising very early. He drinks coffee, shaves, and showers, while I stretch out in bed to get a few more minutes of sleep. But one morning, I am wakened by strange sounds coming from the kitchen.

At first all I can make out are low rumblings, like my dog growling in his sleep, but it isn't that. I can hear furious whispered words, the spat-out mutterings of a person highly agitated. I get out of bed silently and creep down the hall, like a thief in my own home. I feel a buzzing in my head, an angry hornet, an alarm going off, and each tiptoe closer to the kitchen causes it to steadily rise in pitch. I can hear him clearly now, his seething one-sided conversation: "What do you want from me?"

Silence.

"Get out of here!"

Silence.

"Who are you? Reveal yourself!"

Silence.

"Get the fuck out of here before I blow your head off."

My insides collapse, as if all the strands and sinews holding muscle to bone suddenly disintegrate. I have nothing in me that knows how to handle a situation like this. I stumble into the kitchen. His appearance shocks me. He is rougher than I've ever seen him. Unshaven and wild, greasy hair. And his eyes, like two huge black tornadoes.

He sees my fear and instantly softens, puts on his gentle-eyed face and reins in the beast. "I'm sorry I look so bad, darling, I thought you were asleep," he says.

"I heard you talking to someone," I say.

"I wasn't talking to anyone. There's no one here but me and you."

"Yes, you were definitely very angry with someone."

"Oh that? That was nothing. Please don't worry about it."

"But you scared me."

"You don't need to be scared. I'm just protecting us, darling."

"Protecting us from what?"

"Well, you know I communicate with angels, right? I can only do that because I'm very pure of soul. You might think of me as a soldier of light. And as a soldier of light, I sometimes have to do battle with evil entities that want to destroy us."

I stare hard at him. I feel a little stitch in my brain pop. This is the first time he has ever told me his communications have such a dark side to them. "Destroy us?"

"Yes, darling, I was hoping I wouldn't have to tell you this, but your friends and family have been sending demons to attack me."

"But why? Why do you think they're doing that?"

"Because they don't want us to be together."

Isaac Newton Falls in Love

Despite being twenty-two years older, he falls in love with me immediately. Falls endlessly in a circle like an orbiting satellite. His heart does rolling dives.

Constellations rise and fall, he keeps his age hidden from me for as long as he can, the planets only seem to wander. Locked in an embrace, two galaxies will collide.

He insists that I do not have much contact with my mother and father and three brothers. Stars swarm like bees to the most violent places in the cosmos, where my understanding of the laws of physics stops.

This is because he has met my family, and he is convinced they have secrets. Secrets they need to bring out into the open. Unrelenting, I am bent and curved out of shape by his every moon and sun.

He believes they are hiding years of sexual abuse, and he wants them to admit it. He that gouges out vast canyons, he that shapes continents, he that sculpts beacons in me will eventually crush me.

But there is no basis in reality for his belief. He is completely wrong, and my family is very upset.

The gravity of this scares me. And still, this is where I want to be: the border of the known and the unknown, end of the universe.

Seven

He peers out the window and sees a thick gloom. It's like an opaque gel coats everything, interferes with the way the light refracts back into his eyes, makes things look muddy and matte. And though he rarely leaves his elderly mother's tiny apartment, there is always a strange gritty substance covering his boots. His stomach feels green and sour, his throat, powdered with dust. He believes he is a shaman experiencing a kundalini awakening and must fast to achieve purity, and become more attuned to the spirit world.

DAY 1-2: Low blood sugar. Slowed heart rate and reduced blood pressure. Headaches, dizziness, nausea, glazed eyes, heavily coated tongue. Intense hunger.

He spends most of the first two days trying to read, but gives up when the print slips off the pages as if it was sand. Supine, staring at the ceiling, he wafts in and out of a dead man's sleep. He has a dream he is sitting across from an elegant and slender European psychiatrist. Wearing black and yellow, she reminds him of a very stylish bee. She stares at him, the corners of her mouth turned down like the sheets on a bed he wants to lie in. "You are no better than a banana," she says, and takes a bite of her apple.

DAY 3-7: Oily, pallid complexion. Ketones detected in urine and blood. Desire to eat disappears. Exhaustion. Old injuries become irritated and painful. Muscles become tight and sore due to toxin irritation.

He aches all over, knees and lower back especially. His slumping heart rate is of much neurotic preoccupation – it beats more slowly, but with a stronger thud. Weakness magnifies and saturates even micro-movements, like the bending of a wrist, or inflation of lungs, the tangled chain of muscle contractions for swallowing with an Adam's apple turned goldfish.

Someone slides a piece of paper under the door. Stumbly brained, he reads it: *The stars have magic to give you. Don't close your eyes.* Who sent this? He closes his eyes.

DAY 8-14: The lymphatic system expels mucoid matter through the nose or throat. Basal metabolic rate is greatly reduced. Overwhelming anxiety. Extreme weakness persists. Insomnia sets in.

So cold, he spends most hours hunched beside the radiator, layered in blankets. His stomach evolves from feeling like the emptiness of an inside-out pocket, wrinkled and redundant, to the fullest ferocity of a blazing supernova giving birth to a black hole. He would not have been surprised to look down at the flesh of his concave abdomen and see instead the wet round portal to another universe.

He notices another note. He moves over to it, steering his body like a tired mule, churning his limbs through the crush of air that presses down on him like water at the bottom of the sea. It says: *Welcome your truest desires. Don't close your eyes.*

Standing there, contemplating the words, he feels a strange fullness come into his mouth. His tongue rubs the inside of his cheek and he remembers kissing someone once, her mouth and his like two salmon spawning. Suddenly lightheaded, he sees the note dissolving into sparkly stars.

DAY 15-21: More energy and clarity of mind. Tongue is pink and breath is fresh.

Inch by inch, his body changes from heavy dry wood to an eel of supple light. Moving around the apartment, he feels boneless, like a loose assemblage of seaweed. He gazes at his wet, smooth hands, suddenly foreign to him, and feels tenderly moved by all they have done for him. His fingers flutter to another letter: *You can travel freely into the next world. Don't close your eyes.* The handwriting is familiar; it could pass for his own.

The vision quest starts now. He gives up wearing clothes when he sees flames leaping from his body. His skin so hot, he feels the fabric might spontaneously combust on contact. Even the slightest sense of hair, soft against his forehead, drenches him in spasms of unbearable burning sweetness.

DAY 22-30: Body works at maximum capacity to replace damaged tissue. Memory and concentration improve. The eyes become bright.

He goes through spells of unidentifying with the human shape. His pulse has become normal in rhythm and time, but his heart is an eye and it pumps and blinks with the ebb and flow of ocean tides.

He leaves the apartment now, comes and goes as he pleases. Today he wants to be a ripe orange in love with the lissome limb from which he grows, out of nothing, into everything.

He meets a girl, wearing only the sky, she comes and plucks him and rolls his warmth into the palms of her hands. She peels him like a steamed stamp off a love letter from very far away. She bites into a mouthful of his pulp, his sweet marrow, and feels his fine, full-grown juice drip softly down her chin. Or maybe he is the sky and she, wearing only him, comes and feeds the orange to the stars.

*

His spirituality takes a decidedly Christian turn. He comes to believe he is a prophet who can speak in tongues and channel Archangel Michael and the Holy Spirit. To make his marriage sacred in the eyes of God, he remarries his wife in the Catholic Church. His gratefulness knows no limits. He writes letter after letter:

Dear Father Joe,

Thank you, from the depths of our hearts for marrying us, for your compassion and grace, your time and patience, and your understanding of the true light of God. I sought out St. Mary's for Leah and me to come together with Jesus and his unconditional love that blazes in his heart, and since then we have found ourselves at home in your company, and amongst all the members of the parish. To all those at St. Mary's, bless you and thanks. And thank you to the Blessed Mary Mother of God, St. Joseph, and to Our Lord.
Respectfully yours,
Tony

Dear Frances and Keith,

There you were, two of the most beautiful loving people, celebrating the anniversary of your first date on the day of our marriage: two beginnings, poetically coming together in God's grace. Your lives, your wisdom, your journey together, suddenly became our guiding light as you witnessed our own spiritual journey. How wonderful that you would be so generous to make this effort to yet again be here for us. Glorious ambassadors of God you truly are. We love you. You are God's love, as you were that day in Toronto and as you are here again for our marriage at St. Mary's in Kingston. We will always treasure your kindness, and proudly echo it to all. In a world of cold indifference, how joyous to bask in the warmth of your dignity, loyalty, and eternal, divine good nature. Our home will

always be your home, and we will always be here for you and your family whenever you need us.
Sincerely yours,
Tony

Never having been confirmed in the Catholic Church as a child, he receives the sacrament as an adult, and feels as though he has paved a path to the Father with Jesus' white light as his guide. But his newfound Catholicism becomes an obsession. The more pure he feels he becomes, the more susceptible he is to evil attack. Holy water must be used as often as possible to drive away dark forces.

TONY'S HOLY WATER BLESSING

IN THE NAME OF THE FATHER AND THE SON AND THE HOLY SPIRIT, I USE THIS HOLY WATER TO CAST OUT ALL DEMON SPIRITS OR DISCARNATE SPIRITS OR DARKNESS OF ANY KIND FROM OURSELVES, OUR HOME, OUR ANIMALS, AND OUR WORLDLY POSSESSIONS, AND SEND THEM TO HELL OR THE NETHERWORLD SO THAT WE MAY ALL BE AS GOD INTENDED US TO BE: HIS MOST BEAUTIFUL CREATIONS. WE PRAY THAT THE FATHER, THE SON, AND THE HOLY SPIRIT PROTECT US.

If the spirits are particularly dark, stronger language is necessary.

TONY'S HOLY WATER EXORCISM FOR DARKER SPIRITS

I USE THIS HOLY WATER TO CAST OUT AND DAMN TO HELL ALL EVIL SPIRITS AND DEMONS

AND THOSE WHO SEND THEM. I USE THIS HOLY WATER TO CAST OUT AND DAMN TO HELL ALL EVIL PEOPLE WORKING AGAINST US. I USE THIS HOLY WATER TO CAST OUT AND DAMN TO HELL EACH AND EVERY ONE OF THEIR SOULS. AND I PRONOUNCE A CURSE ON ALL THESE NOXIOUS VERMIN AND I PRAY THAT THE FATHER, THE SON, AND THE HOLY SPIRIT JUDGE THEM AND PUNISH THEM HARSHLY WITH FIRE UNTIL THEY ARE OBLITERATED.

And the spirits do get darker, and he channels less about the beauty of God's love, and more about sexual perversions and murder. He is fixated on Satanic ritual abuse, convinced that his wife's parents are master practitioners who have drank and bathed in the blood of the hundreds of babies and children they have molested, tortured and sacrificially killed. His terrified wife is left to wonder, *Why are all these sickening things constantly on his mind? What is he capable of? Is he dangerous?*
And the attacks get stronger, coming not only from hell and the netherworld but from the astral realms as well. So he continues his damnations and fervent pleas for protection, until one day he has the revelation that Christianity is nothing but a massive conspiracy to cover up pedophilia and incest. Because Adam and Eve must have populated the earth by having sex with their children, and their children must have had sex with each other, and so on. "That's it," he says. "We are through with Catholicism! We renounce our sacraments and reclaim our souls."
His wife follows him, not because she agrees, but because she has learned the hard way that she has no choice. "A wife must support her husband one hundred percent," he says. "A wife is not allowed to disagree with her husband. That's just the way it is."
He pours the holy water down the drain, and destroys all his crucifixes and rosaries in hopes of finally silencing his invisible

enemies. But the attacks keep boiling in his brain, increasing in power and frequency – no longer in possession of his soul, the beings become more frantic in their efforts to capture and return it to the very darkest demon, the one in charge of all Christianity, Satan himself. They bombard him with negative energy and horrible accusations. They say he is a rapist, he is a child molester, they say he is going to harm his family. He turns to a cosmic, New Age Father-Mother God for comfort. Many times during the day and night he shouts to his unseen assailants, "Leave us alone! We've renounced our faith! We are not Catholic anymore." Yet they are always there, in his head. He openly bickers and fights with them, threatens them with mutilation and death.

who are you
what kind of being are you
reveal yourself
you demon spirit
astral attacker
leave me
leave this room
or I'll kill you
my fist like a train
through your skull
your brains coming out red
the other side of the tunnel
my knife in your stomach
guts pumping out
I can smell the dog stink
of your liver, spleen
intestines

*

MOST BEAUTIFUL FATHER-MOTHER GOD
I HONOUR YOU I THANK YOU FOR YOUR
BLESSINGS I AM SO GRATEFUL PLEASE
I PRAY YOU SAVE ME PROTECT ME
MY OWN HEART IS PURE

*

who are you
reveal yourself
you astral attacker
leave this room
or I'll slice you
clean through the jugular
your throat a cup

filling with blood
'til I sever your head entirely
peel back the skin of your face
scrape past muscle to the bone
turn your head upside down
like a bowl
eat your skull meat
your still wet tongue
I can taste the dread
in your eyeballs
bursting fish eggs
in my jaws

*

MOST BENEFICENT FATHER-MOTHER GOD
HAVE MERCY ON ME IN MY TIME OF NEED
I GIVE MYSELF OVER TO YOU
AND YOUR INFINITE KINDNESS
MY SOUL IS UNSTAINED

Eight

March 15, 2006

HER MAJESTY THE QUEEN V. ANTONIO ROSATO

CHARGE: Criminal Harassment

PRELIMINARY INQUIRY continued.

EXAMINATION-IN-CHIEF BY MS. CHRISTIE

MS. CHRISTIE: Was there any other behaviour on Mr. Rosato's part that suggested to you that perhaps all was not well mentally for him?

LEAH MURRAY: Yes. He went through everything, all my belongings, and he destroyed anything he thought was inappropriate. He went through all my photo albums and threw out all the pictures with people in them, because he thought I might look at these pictures lustfully. He also went through all my clothes, and destroyed anything he thought might be slightly sexy or revealing.

Q. With respect to the photos that he destroyed, did you consent to their destruction?

A. Well, at first I told him I didn't want him to destroy them because it wasn't necessary, because these things he was saying about them weren't true. But he kept at it. He wouldn't drop it. And so just to make things easier, I finally thought to myself, *Is it really that important that I have this picture of a friend who I haven't seen in fifteen years? No. I'll just let him do it. If it makes him happy, I will let him do what he wants.*

Q. When you say that he kept at it, can you describe his behaviour? What would he say, what would he do, how close was he to you?

A. It felt like an interrogation. There would be times, when, for hours at a time, sometimes all night long, he would be interrogating me and badgering me, just constantly in my face.

Q. And how did that interrogation make you feel?

A. Terrified, and I'd be exhausted and confused, and I'd be crying, and it would just go on and on and on.

Q. With respect to the clothing he destroyed, was it clothing you had purchased for yourself?

A. Yes.

Q. Can you describe the clothing?

A. Just regular skirts and dresses.

Q. What would he do with them?

A. He would tear them up. He was concerned about people going through the garbage and finding them, so he just destroyed them.

Q. What was the reason he gave you for destroying your clothing?

A. He said I wasn't allowed to wear them anymore because I looked slutty in them, and because they contained energy – trapped deviant energy from all the horrible things he accused me of doing, like being in gangbangs with hundreds of men, raping young girls, being a prostitute and a stripper, having phone sex behind his back, having sex with anybody who might have come into my apartment. He asked me once if any man had ever been in my apartment, and I said, "Well, the landlord," and so automatically he thought I must have had sex with the landlord.

Q. Was there any basis for those assertions on his part?

A. No.

Q. Was there anything else that he destroyed of yours?

A. He destroyed a lot of keepsakes that were given to me by my family. He believed my family had cursed them. Jewellery that my mother had given me, he threw that out. And I had a doll collection that my mother had given me. He made me rip their heads off.

Q. Can you describe how he was able to exert that kind of control, to have you in fact destroy your own dolls?

A. He would just wear me down. He would yell at me, he would lecture me, he would call me names, he would say I was a terrible person – the only way I was ever going to be worth anything was if I listened to him and did what he told me to do.

Q. And so as a result of that pressure, you destroyed your own doll collection.

A. Yes, because it was the only way to make him stop. It was the only way he would be happy with me.

Q. Can you describe your emotional, mental, and physical response to that badgering?

A. I lost all my self-esteem and all my confidence. I felt desperate, and I felt very depressed, and sad, and hopeless. I felt exhausted. I felt like my spirit was broken.

Things Given Up or Destroyed Upon Threat of Consequences (Up to and Including Death)

CDs
This music you listen to is so uninspiring. I only want the best for you, so would you mind letting me go through your collection? I'll let you keep the most appropriate ones.

Books
What's wrong with you? Why do you have so many books with dark subject matter? I care deeply about you and I'm starting to get worried. Do you have some kind of sick mind?

Makeup
Get a tissue and come over here. You better wipe off that lipstick. You look so hard in makeup. I love you, darling, and no wife of mine is going to go around looking like some cheap whore.

Photos of Ex-Boyfriends
It hurts me that you still have these, darling. Now that you're with me, would you please honour our relationship by removing these from your albums? You promised you would start over fresh for me.

Handmade Hope Chest
Your mother had this made for you? It looks like a coffin! This is a curse. Your mother is wishing death on you. Your family, honest to God, wants you to die. I won't have this in my home. It's gone.

Clothing
These skirts are awful! They would make a prostitute blush! Did you wear these with your boyfriends? How dare you wear these clothes around me! You're trying to contaminate me with your degradation, aren't you?

Grandfather's Antique Fiddle

Your grandfather gave this to you? Don't you know what fiddling really means? He's trying to send you a message but you're too stupid to figure it out. Your grandfather wants to fiddle with *you*. I'm going to smash this into a thousand pieces to protect you, and teach that old pervert a lesson.

Childhood Photos of Friends

Oh my God, this photo is sick. Look at the expression on your friend's face. How old is she here? Nine? What do you think her look says? Or are you that much of an idiot you can't figure it out? Her look says: "I'm naughty, I'm a lesbian and I want to fuck you." You can't keep this, darling. You're a lesbian if you want to keep this.

Computer

What? This used to belong to your ex-fiancé? How dare you not tell me until now? This must be destroyed. We're going to smash the insides and then send him back the empty metal carcass as a warning. Besides, it's inappropriate for someone as depraved as you to have access to the Internet. No matter how much you deny it, I'm certain you're getting off on lesbian porn when I'm not around and I won't stand for that. Time to own up to all your lies.

Veterinary Care for Ferret

Your ferret didn't die of cancer. Your ferret died because she was forced to absorb your negative energy. You're a terrible person who's never done anything good in her life. Look at my life. I've been a good, upstanding citizen and I've helped people at every opportunity. What have you got to show for your life? You've lived nothing but a dirty, nasty existence. You've accomplished nothing. And now you've gone and killed your ferret. All that black shit that came out her eyes and her mouth? That's all your perversion right there.

Friends

You're fucking all your friends behind my back. And they're all going to give you AIDS. Spare me the pathetic excuses, you whore! How do I know? Archangel Michael told me. So if you say it's not true, it means you're calling either me or Archangel Michael a liar. What's it going to be, you slut? Don't you deny it, or else you're going to burn in hell for your betrayals. If you don't agree to stop seeing your friends right now, I'm going to leave you and tell everyone you're insane. You don't deserve someone as beneficent as me. I'm a star and you're nothing but a star fucker. Give me your wedding ring. You're not worthy to wear it. No one would ever want to marry an asshole like you.

Family

Your family members are nothing but a sick gang of pedophiles and Satan worshippers. You're fucking your brothers and your father and your grandfather, and I swear to God they're trying to kill you and steal our baby. They're using their black magic on you to confuse you and turn you against me. Can't you see? Are you so fucking stupid? *I'm* the one who loves you. *I'm* the one who's protecting you. Stop crying, you pathetic moron! You make me sick with your lack of faith. *I'm* your husband and you do as I say. I forbid every single member of your family from ever seeing my child after it's born. And if they ever try to kidnap you, so help me God, I will kill them. And if I ever find out that you're seeing them behind my back, I promise you'll die, too.

Nine

March 15, 2006

HER MAJESTY THE QUEEN V. ANTONIO ROSATO

CHARGE: Criminal Harassment

PRELIMINARY INQUIRY continued.

EXAMINATION-IN-CHIEF BY MS. CHRISTIE continued.

MS. CHRISTIE: I'd like you to make reference to any acts of a sexual nature that you participated in without consenting during the course of your marriage to Mr. Rosato.

LEAH MURRAY: He said he was having clairvoyant visions, and he could clairvoyantly see me engaging in sexually deviant acts. I of course denied it because it wasn't true; I did not do those things. But that just made him angry, and then he forced me to do those things with him.

Q. Did you consent to any of these sexual acts?

A. I did not want to do them.

Q. Did you convey that to Mr. Rosato?

A. Yes, I said, "I don't want to do these things," and I was crying and I was upset.

Q. What was his response to what you said and your emotional state?

A. He would get angry. He said he was upset that I would do these things with other people but not with him. He would say, "If you truly loved me, then you would do these things. If you really trusted me, then you would do these things."

And I would continue to say, "I've never done these things, I don't want to do these things, I can't do these things." But he would not let up. He would just keep on bullying me, saying the same things again and again.

It would reach a point where it had gone on for hours, where he would keep me up all night long with the constant, "I know you did this, you're just repressing the memories, you're just hiding it from me," over and over, trying to coerce me, and I just couldn't take it anymore. I felt completely exhausted and confused and tormented, and it became not even a choice anymore. That was the only way it was going to stop.

Q. By participating?

A. Yes.

The Domestic Captor's Handbook

Part 1: How To Destroy Another Human Being in 10 Easy Steps

1.
woo her
by whirlwind courtship
        (shower her
        with praise, gifts
        and affection)

2.
isolate her
from her community
and support systems
        (eliminate her
        friends first
        then family)

3.
weaken her
with arbitrary rules
        (torment her
        with random rage)

4.
control her
by deciding
who she sees
what she wears
when she sleeps
where she goes
and how much she eats

5.
confuse her
by shaming and terrorizing her
while also
claiming to love her

6.
deprive her
of sentimental belongings
     (make her
     willingly destroy them)

7.
victimize her
with constant psychological abuse
     (threaten her
     intimidate her)

8.
coerce her
into humiliating
sexual acts

9.
bully her
into rejecting
her dearest loved ones

10.
force her
to denounce
her most fundamental beliefs

Part 2: Three Helpful Hints

A.
All it takes to get nine hundred and thirteen people to follow
you,
   to leave their homes,
   to love you like a god,
   to commit mass suicide,
is to make them feel special.

B.
All it takes to strip search a female fast-food restaurant worker,
   to confine her in the bathroom,
   to make her dance naked and do jumping jacks,
   to slap her buttocks and force her to perform lewd acts,
is to identify yourself as a police officer.

C.
All it takes to make a person admit to something they did not
do,
   to force them into betraying their friends and family,
   to pressure them into lying about the past,
   to coerce them into writing down a false confession,
is to offer them rewards like sleep, food, or stopping the
interrogation.

Interrogation Techniques Recommended/Approved by US Officials (and My Ex-Husband)

1. Direct, straightforward questions
2. Yelling at detainee
3. Incentive or removal of incentive
4. Playing on detainee's love for a particular group
5. Significantly increasing fear level of detainee
6. Reducing fear level of detainee
7. Boosting the ego of detainee
8. Insulting the ego of detainee
9. Invoking feelings of futility in detainee
10. Convincing detainee interrogator knows all
11. Continually repeating same questions to detainee during same interrogation period
12. Convincing detainee interrogator has damning/inaccurate file, which must be fixed
13. Good cop, bad cop
14. Rapid-fire questioning with no time for answer
15. Staring at detainee to encourage discomfort
16. Dietary manipulation
17. Isolating prisoner for up to 30 days
18. Prolonged interrogations (e.g. 20 hours)
19. Removal of comfort items
20. Removal of detainee's clothing
21. Sleep deprivation
22. Threat of imminent death to detainee or her family members

Ten

March 15, 2006

HER MAJESTY THE QUEEN V. ANTONIO ROSATO

CHARGE: Criminal Harassment

PRELIMINARY INQUIRY continued.

<u>**EXAMINATION-IN-CHIEF BY MS. CHRISTIE**</u>
<u>**continued.**</u>

MS. CHRISTIE: So following your marriage at City Hall, you resumed your life in Kingston, and he continued to live with his mother in Toronto.

LEAH MURRAY: Yes.

Q. How often would you see him following your marriage?

A. On weekends.

Q. What kind of contact did you have when he wasn't visiting you in Kingston?

A. He would call me anywhere from four to ten times a day, depending on his mood. He was checking up on me, wanting to know where I was, exactly what I had done that day, exactly what I was going to be doing later.

Q. Did he ever give you any directions when he phoned you in terms of what you could or could not do?

A. Yes, he would tell me, "I don't want you speaking to your parents today. I don't want you to go outside. I want you to do this. I want you to eat that." Everything.

Q. Did you comply with those requests?

A. Yes.

Q. And why did you do so when he wasn't present in the same city?

A. Because at that point I was so scared. I couldn't lie to him. If he said, "I want you to eat an entire piece of chicken for dinner," and if I only ate half, I would say, "I only ate half." I was so afraid he'd know it if I was lying.

Q. What were you afraid would happen?

A. He would get angry.

Q. Okay, so I'm trying to understand, given his geographic distance from you, if you chose to eat half, he clearly wouldn't have known you hadn't eaten the other half, correct?

A. Right.

Q. So I'm trying to understand your fear level.

A. He just had that kind of control over me.

Dingy kitchen, morning. A woman, twenty-seven, five months pregnant, sits at the table. She looks sick and worried. A man, forty-nine, busily prepares a large breakfast. He cooks huge portions of eggs and toast, and oatmeal with fruit. He sets it down in front of her.

MAN: Eat this.

WOMAN: I can't eat this.

MAN: You're going to eat this, darling.

WOMAN: But I feel so sick. You don't understand.

MAN: Oh I understand. I understand perfectly well. I understand if you can take on a hundred men in a gangbang, then you can eat your fucking breakfast.

WOMAN: [*Crying.*] Oh my God.

MAN: [*Loud, angry.*] What?

WOMAN: [*Quiet, hopeless.*] Nothing. [*She takes a few bites and more tears well up.*] I can't eat this.

MAN: [*Glowering, speaking low, through clenched teeth.*] You will sit here until you eat every last bit of this breakfast. I don't care how long it takes. I'm not letting you up until this plate is empty. [*He puts his hands firmly on her shoulders, preventing her from rising. He stays like this, unmoving, for a full thirty minutes – the length of time it takes for the woman to choke back as much breakfast as she can. There's no sound except for the woman occasionally gagging. Finally, she pushes the plate away.*]

WOMAN: [*Still tearful, she looks up at him.*] I'm sorry, that's as much as I can eat.

MAN: [*Smiling.*] Good girl. I'm proud of you. I love you. [*He releases his grip on her shoulders and opens his arms wide to embrace her.*]

WOMAN: [*Stands up, exhausted, defeated, lets herself be hugged.*] I love you, too.

March 15, 2006

HER MAJESTY THE QUEEN V. ANTONIO ROSATO

CHARGE: Criminal Harassment

PRELIMINARY INQUIRY continued.

EXAMINATION-IN-CHIEF BY MS. CHRISTIE continued.

MS. CHRISTIE: Can you give me any more examples of the types of things he would direct you to do or not to do?

LEAH MURRAY: Everything. It was what movies I was allowed to watch, what music I was allowed to listen to. When he still believed in the Catholic Church, he even told me I needed to get baptized. I was always supposed to be saying certain prayers and doing cleansing and purifying rituals, using holy water. He would tell me to do all those things.

Q. Did you in fact get baptized in the Catholic Church?

A. Yes.

Q. It was Mr. Rosato's idea?

A. Yes.

Q. What did Mr. Rosato tell you was the reason he wanted you to be baptized?

A. He said I was impure. I was so filthy from all my sins, I needed to be cleansed and purified, and baptism was the only way.

February 18, 2005

To: Tina Tom

Re: Leah Murray

Prior Relationship:
None, until early 2004. I met Tony and Leah in January. Tony introduced Leah to a group I was and still am part of, conducted through St. Mary's Cathedral: The RCIA (The Rite of Christian Initiation of Adults).

Leah asked me if I would be her sponsor, and later on, her godmother. On Saturday, April 10, 2004, Leah was received into the Catholic Church.

We met on occasion for the next few months in a group setting until she and Tony moved away to Toronto.

I did not contact them by phone, for I did not have their phone number.

Leah phoned me sometime in the fall. I felt she was under stress, I could hear it in her voice. She explained to me that she and Tony had reviewed the Catholic Catechism and felt the Catholic faith did not meet their needs, that it was a religion empty of love. My response was that God loves us and gives each and every one of us the freedom to choose. And as her godmother, I reminded Leah that she made the choice to become Catholic as an adult. She was not forced to do this by any of us, and I encouraged her to search her heart for the truth.

I told her I would pray for her and reminded her that God loves her. I was not angry – shocked by her decision, yes – but deep down I did not believe this was Leah's choice.

The Phone Call:
On Wednesday, October 13, 2004, at approximately 9:30 AM, I received a phone call from Tony Rosato at my place of work. He sounded agitated. He proceeded immediately to tell me

how he and Leah were upset with me, and how he did not care for what I had said to Leah in our previous conversation. He started talking about spirits and I had no idea what he meant. It was an uncomfortable and bizarre situation.

He asked me if I believed in spirits. I said I believed in the Holy Spirit. Then with a strange and angry voice he said, "I do not appreciate you sending evil spirits." He said he was seeing evil spirits hovering over his daughter's crib sent there by me, to tell them their souls were condemned and needed to be saved. He kept repeating about evil spirits and told me to stop praying for them.

I just stood there, dumbfounded, in disbelief. If I had not experienced this conversation firsthand, I would never believe someone could think and say such things.

I remained calm and denied everything and tried to reason with him, and reassured him that I would never want to harm Leah, him, and definitely never their daughter. To try to defuse the situation, I simply said I was sorry if he felt this way.

He then said they had left the Catholic Church and Leah did not want me as her godmother, nor did she want me to have any contact with her. I just could not believe what he was saying to me.

He then put Leah on the phone and again I could hear the tension in her voice. She told me, "I do not want you as my godmother." My heart went out to her over the phone, but I knew not to aggravate the situation.

I was very worried for Leah and her daughter, but I made no attempt to contact Leah. I felt she would be in danger, and I did not want to jeopardize her safety, nor her daughter's. I understood Tony was trying to alienate her from any love and support, and that I was a threat to this plan.

Donna D.

Eleven

March 15, 2006

HER MAJESTY THE QUEEN V. ANTONIO ROSATO

CHARGE: Criminal Harassment

PRELIMINARY INQUIRY continued.

EXAMINATION-IN-CHIEF BY MS. CHRISTIE continued.

MS. CHRISTIE: Before your daughter was born in September 2004, was there any other behaviour, or any direction, or any controlling attempts on his part when you were together on a street, or in a social setting?

LEAH MURRAY: He was very concerned about outward appearances, and he wanted it to seem as though we were a perfectly fine, happy couple. So he was always watching me to see what I was doing, or where I was looking, and even what kind of look I had on my face. If somebody, male or female, were to walk in front of me and I happened to look at them, he would accuse me of lusting after that person. He'd say I was having inappropriate sexual thoughts. So I basically just looked down. I was very, very quiet and meek, and I just let him do all the talking all the time.

We are walking along the side of the road. "I need to be tough on you to make you a better person," he says.

I wait twenty seconds. The amount of time it takes blood to circulate throughout the body. Fingertips to toes, bone to skin. I wait twenty seconds before I speak. I need to slowly hatch what I plan to say, go over my sentences, carefully edit and censor, choose the most benign words, jump ahead to how far-fetched he might interpret my meaning.

Five cars go by. Already shrinking, I heave up my eyes to meet his and ask, "But can't you see all you're doing is making me cry?"

"What's wrong with you?" he says. "Why are you in this permanent cringe? You're an embarrassment to me. You're always hunched over, you're always looking down at the ground like some flinching coward. You should hold your head up high, be a proud woman. Besides, you bring it on yourself. I'll stop being tough when you learn to give me the respect I deserve, when you learn to be a proper wife!"

I feel as small as the space between two wrinkles on his angry forehead. More cars go by and I think about that split second when the sound changes from high to low, that instant when the people in the cars catch sight of strangers on the sidewalk as though they were just photographs, frozen in time. "I'm sorry," I say, and we walk on. How many times had I been in one of those cars, gazing out into the world, comforted by the anonymity and possibility of it all, those single, uncomplicated frames of lives, glimpsing just one out of millions and millions of images, just one out of a steady stream of stills, snapping them into my mind like metallic silver exposed to light. How much would I have given to be any one of those other people. We come across a dead crow in the street. Fully intact, it must have been killed only moments ago. Tony puts his hand on his heart like it injures him to see such carnage. I watch as he steps into the middle of the road and picks it up by the wing, its feathers unfurling, like a Chinese fan flung open, and I am struck by the tenderness with which he carries it to the grass. And this one of me becomes a thousand of me, and I wonder what we must look like to those people in the cars passing by. This strange, severe man holding a dead bird, this delicately outspread crow, and this lonely quail of a pregnant girl in a long blue dress.

Night after night, I lie in bed, overcome by worry. Feeling life quicken inside me, I stare up at the starry sky through my open window for sleepless hours that will not let me forget those small specks of light, those millions of clocks, cosmic heartbeats, their lifespans stretched out over trillions of years, devastating me with their relentless flows of time toward their eventual ends and the end of everything.

And so I cannot hide from his accusations forever. I have to placate him when he demands to have blood tests done to make sure he is the real father. I have to calm him down when he becomes concerned that my family or my obstetrician or the people from church want to steal the baby to use her for satanic rituals.

But like a town that was built in the desert once, a hundred years ago, only ghosts live there now. So must I realize the people I once imagined myself and him to be are only ghosts. Because glass shatters, mortar crumbles, and buildings collapse. Because stars cannot shine forever, their ashes swept into emptiness. Because even black holes will disappear, the cosmos becoming nothing but softly fading flakes of light.

And now he wants me to move to Toronto when I am nine months pregnant so I can have the baby there. I am shocked. With only three weeks left, I have already made all the arrangements to have the baby here in Kingston. My obstetrician advises against the move and tells me she is considering calling the Children's Aid. He takes this as a threat and more proof they are trying to steal the baby.

I tell him I am afraid to move, but he gets the last word. He always gets the last word. He makes all the decisions. He finds an apartment, he gets a moving van, he packs everything up himself, and he says, "Okay, you're leaving and you're not telling your parents, and you're not allowed to tell them your new address."

Terrified, I say, "What if something happens? Don't I need to be in touch with my family? What if there's an illness or an accident?" But the most he concedes is that I be allowed to tell them our phone number.

The arrow of time leads to my destruction. The very thing that allows me to live in the first place, because it takes time for matter to form, for gravity to pull the pieces together, is the very thing that causes the universe to become nothing but a sea of embers, slowly drifting toward absolute zero.

So I move, and we find an obstetrician in Toronto and I give birth three weeks later. As each moment passes, things change that can never be undone. My future will be different from my past. In the midst of chaos, I feel a glimmer of something taking shape. The way a sea turtle hauls herself from the ocean and makes her nest on the beach, an attempt to circumvent decay, mortar uncrumbling, buildings uncollapsing, in moonlit sands that glisten like crushed glass, or the cinders of a stelliferous night, I say to him, "I'd really like to call my mother and let my family know she's been born."

But he gets very angry with me. He tells me I am a disgrace. I am a disgusting, disgraceful person to want to associate with criminals like that.

I can hear ghosts breathing.

Then they are gone.

You were swept away into the sea
return to me
return, return, return to me
return

return, return
to me
return to me

wet and wearing seaweed

Sometimes he lets up. Sometimes, out of the darkness, he comes shining through and is the man I want, the man he so many times promises he will be, the man deep down, in moments of lucidity, I know he wishes to be.

It is with this man in mind that I write for our baby a letter describing her birth, and her father's part in it.

Dear daughter,

All this time you are growing inside me, not a minute goes by when I am not wondering who you are. Who is this little person who kicks me, and rolls around, and has hiccups? The realness of you sweeps over me in waves, sometimes gently, like the ocean on a calm day, or sometimes the waves come crashing down on me, the seas heaving and rioting with joy. I know this is the same for your father, when, during our last ultrasound, he says with such excitement, and tears in his eyes, "Leah! You've got a baby inside you!"

We see the profile of your face that day, and though I know you are a part of me, joined to me, it's like I am seeing a stranger's face, a stranger I love more than anything, a stranger I want, more than anything, to know.

So I wait and wait for you to come. The contractions start on September 25, about 4:30 in the morning. As the pains get stronger and closer together, your father tries to make me feel better by timing the contractions, getting me popsicles and grapes, massaging my feet, and playing my Neil Diamond CD for me.

By 2:30 in the afternoon I really want to go to the hospital so we call a taxi. People wish us luck in the elevator, and your father nearly has to carry me to the taxi, and then into the hospital, where he finds me a wheelchair, and takes me to be assessed.

A little while later, once we're settled in our room, I am given an epidural. The nurse keeps telling me to sleep, but I am too excited. Your father is too excited to sleep, too, so he holds my hand. I am also a little scared, so I ask him to keep on holding my hand, to not let go, and to watch over me if I close my eyes, and he does.

The nurse keeps the volume of your heart rate monitor turned up so we can listen to your heart, and make sure it keeps beating strongly. Each beat fills me with awe, and brings me closer to the time when you and I will meet.

At midnight, the nurse says you are almost ready to arrive. That's when I am truly struck by the realization that you will be here so soon, after such a long time of waiting and hoping. I am so happy and nervous and thrilled and scared, wanting everything to be okay. All I care about is your safe delivery.

When it's time for me to start pushing, your father puts his mouth close to my ear and whispers words of encouragement. All the nurses and doctors are trying to say and do helpful things to make you come out. And you do!

At 2:41 AM on September 26, 2004, you are born. Our baby. Our very own baby. You.

The first thing I notice is how absolutely perfect you are in every way. You are so clean, and your skin is a beautiful colour of pink. You have lots of dark hair, and the sweetest, roundest little face. Your eyes are wide-open, and your lips slightly pursed.

You don't cry. In fact, you seem so calm the nurse takes you over to the baby warmer to make sure you're healthy. Your father goes with you, and I watch him watching you. He looks so concerned, like he has all the care in the world in his eyes for you. When you do start to cry, he says, "Oh baby, it's okay!"

I keep asking if you're all right. I am so impatient to hold you! Finally, the nurse brings you over to me. All your father and I want to do is admire your beauty. We hold you and look at you, and we are astounded by how tiny and perfect you are.

I notice right away that you have your father's ears, and also his chin and eyebrows. Your father points out that you have my eyes and forehead and nose. And I keep thinking, so this is who has been growing inside me, kicking and moving around. I loved you all that time and now you are finally here, for me to love for the rest of my life.

I am so happy, but also so tired. I ask your father if he can hold you while I close my eyes. So he holds you in the chair next to me, and he gazes at you with so much tenderness.

You are so quiet that first night, and you make the most delicate little noises, like little bird noises. And over and over again that night we are amazed by you, by your hands and your feet, your soft skin, and your gentleness.

And all the unknowingness of you is gone, because now you are here, as though you were always here, and there never was a time when you were not.

All my love forever,

Mama

**Her arm is a delicate spiral,
a masterpiece of human flesh.**

Already defined, like length of eyelash,
parabolic curve of earlobe,
all before she was a drop of protoplasm
or even a sparkle,
and before that, too.
When in anticipation of shape,
there was shapelessness,
not particle, nor wave,
occupying less space than gravity,
light, or dreams,
and the unformed wish
more sweeping than all the nebulae put together,
trembled itself into matter.

Twelve

March 15, 2006

HER MAJESTY THE QUEEN V. ANTONIO ROSATO

CHARGE: Criminal Harassment

PRELIMINARY INQUIRY continued.

EXAMINATION-IN-CHIEF BY MS. CHRISTIE continued.

MS. CHRISTIE: Following the birth of your baby, you continued to live with Mr. Rosato until January 2005. Can you describe some of your experiences during that period? If I could take you to Christmas 2004.

LEAH MURRAY: He got extremely paranoid and preoccupied with the attacks. He was constantly shouting at the voices, carrying on conversations. And he was barely sleeping. I could hear him all night long, yelling and rambling and mumbling. He was also convinced the police had taken an apartment in the building across from us to spy on him. He believed his life was in danger.

Q. Did Mr. Rosato describe to you an evolving role he was having in this realm of spirituality?

A. Yes. He would talk for hours on end about how he had been chosen as the most beautiful person in the cosmos, and he was going to save the planet with his light information. He believed he had created a new spirit world. He called it the Universal Soldier spirit world and he was trying to help people get there, specifically Elvis Presley and John Lennon.

Q. Was he ever involved in any kind of media presentation of his ideas?

A. He was trying to set something up. He was trying to contact Oprah and Ron Howard and Jim Carrey. He wanted to have a press conference where he would announce to the world he had information to save the planet.

Q. What made you think you were truly in danger?

A. When he was changing the baby's diaper and he said he had thoughts of sexual molestation implanted in his brain. And right before I left, he burst into the bedroom in the middle of the night, naked, looking completely deranged. He said the astral attackers had implanted a post-hypnotic suggestion in his brain that he was going to harm us.
And there was another thing. He had a cat that was very old, and she was dying, and he said to me, "I think I'm going to drop her off the balcony."
I was stunned. I said, "Why?"
He said, "Well, it will be a way to quicken her death."
And I said, "We should take her to a vet! Vets are the people who take care of that sort of thing." But he did not want to do that. I talked him out of dropping her off the balcony and she ended up dying naturally. But he kept her body, and he would move it around to different places in the apartment. He would cover it up with the baby's blanket and put her toys around it. I left five days after that cat died and her body was still there.

Who am I?

Somehow set apart
from all other things
the light bounces off.
Somehow permanently creased
into the blanket of your brainfolds.

And still, who am I?

A bloodhound
who smells you
very faint or far away.

A catfish
who tastes you
before being inside my mouth.

A cricket
who feels your footfalls,
like earthquakes
between my eardrums.

But even a one-celled organism
senses too hot, too cold,
too poisonous.
It turns
and goes
the other way.

I migrate to that spot
devoid of rods or cones,
my warm-bloodedness unfelt
by your tongue
or bones.

Another night in the smoke-filled bedroom, the windows shut tight, the door held fast. Begging for some fresh air, not for my sake, but for the baby's, the risk of Sudden Infant Death Syndrome weighs heavy on me like the thick smell of burning sage and sweetgrass. But pleading with him never works, it only angers him, incites him, proves to him that I have no faith in his healing rituals, that I've turned against him, just like everyone else. "You need to be cleansed and purified," he says to me.

He keeps the sage and sweetgrass always burning to banish the negative energies plaguing him. Lighting the smudge sticks on the stove elements, he forgets to turn them off, and I walk into the kitchen to find them glowing bright orange. He clutches the wailing baby against his shoulder with one hand, holds his smudge stick in the other, and shouts obscenities to his supernatural foes with his mouth so close to her ear, I worry for her newborn eardrums. But imploring him to stop leads only to louder and more vulgar threats. "This uptight little bitch needs to hear it," he says to me.

He has no patience with her, and believes she cries to purposely annoy him. "Shut up!" he says to her. He is convinced I am poisoning her against him, and accuses her of maliciously attempting to scratch his eyes out. Wanting to discipline her, he forces her to cry face down in her crib. "She needs to respect her father," he says to me. And later, hovering over her, I catch him accusing her of weakness, blaming her for making him more vulnerable to astral attacks. He tells me she has no personality, her birthmark is ugly, and she has demons all around her, demons he has to speak to regularly. "You're dead, I've killed your soul," he says to them.

He supplements his sage and sweetgrass arsenal with crystals and semi-precious stones. Many of the crystals and stones are tiny, some half an inch or smaller, some the size of a pea, and he puts them in her crib and tucks them into her clothing. He also wraps protective necklaces around her neck. I am desperately afraid she will choke or strangle, but again my fears are met with rage, "Your doubts are disgusting," he says to me. He continues to smudge the baby often, and once, I notice burning embers falling onto her head. Glancing up at him with a worried look on my face sends him into a fury. "Don't you dare look at me that way! I know what you're thinking. You don't trust me! You don't have any confidence in my abilities. Well, your lack of faith will destroy this family!" Wrapping the baby tightly in my arms, I run into the bathroom and lock the door. "Are you crying in front of the mirror? You're risking both your lives if I catch you crying in front of the mirror," he says to me.

My cheeks, red and tear-streaked, and nothing left to do but attempt to pacify him, I leave the baby on the bathmat and open the door. He takes a giant step towards me, pushing his face into mine. "Do you want me to get brutal with you? Because I'll get brutal with you! How dare you use that mirror to summon astral attackers! It's your family attacking me, isn't it? Let me tell you, if you ever leave me and go back to your family, serious harm will come to you. And if you don't do exactly as I say, death will come to you."

So I do exactly as he says. The hours inching by, days and nights pass as though time has melded into one endless marathon of minutes, and all I can do is watch him, listen to him with constant carefulness, and never ever let the baby out of my sight.

Until one day, as I am pacing the hallway with the baby, trying to soothe her colic, he casually smokes a homemade sage cigarette and admits that he shook her once while I was in the shower. My heart stops.

Quickly, quickly, I ask him how hard did he shake her? He says he gave her a quick shake, like a little jolt, because she was crying and would not stop. He says he did it in hopes of snapping her out of her crying spell. I need to know more. I ask him if he picked her up and shook her back and forth. He says no, he grabbed her by the shoulders and gave her a quick shake while she was still in her crib. I tell him he could have given her brain damage or even killed her if the shaking had been more severe. He looks unfazed and blows a breathful of sage smoke into the baby's face.

This is it. I feel a fierce ache in my neck. I feel like I am going to vomit. I feel the world collapsing around me like pillars falling on my head, the stars like bits of shrapnel, I feel the universe jolting *me* by the shoulders, dispelling the smoke and dust from my eyes. This is the moment I know I have it in me, despite the threat of death, to somehow, some way, take the baby and run away fast. The cosmos crosses its fingers.

Thirteen

Yesterday he said I was nebulous, I had wasted my life, I had done too many degrading things. Yesterday he could not sleep because dark-energy beings were violating him through the mirrors or anything with a reflection. Yesterday he wore sunglasses all day and night to prevent evil spirits from entering through his eyes.

Today he calls me stupid because I am under astral attack. Today he repeats nonstop his ritualistic banishments and convoluted litanies and prayers. Today clouds with demon faces must be watched carefully.

Three months ago he said I was a failure for having an epidural. Three months ago he forbade me from sending my family a baby picture, convinced that any information about her would help them with their occultist assaults. Three months ago he wanted me to tell everyone I had given birth to a baby boy to confuse them.

Yesterday he said I was a lesbian, a whore, and no better than an animal. Yesterday he demanded complete submission. Yesterday he backed me into a corner and threatened to take my baby away from me forever when I failed to anticipate his demands and broke one of his arbitrary rules.

Today he calls me a bitch for being unsupportive. Today he swings my cat by her tail when she knocks over a vase. Today he says I am a terrible wife for crying and thinking he could ever harm an animal.

Six months ago he said I was feeble and petulant for getting upset when he kicked my dog. Six months ago he claimed my dog was faking being hurt after hitting him with a tree branch. Six months ago he hit me in the small of my back with the same tree branch because I did not believe him.

Yesterday he said I was not allowed to look too long into our baby's eyes for fear I might hypnotize her. Yesterday he lectured me on how I should have had enough intelligence and respect to see that my vacuuming was adding to his suffering. Yesterday he wrote me out a bill for twenty million spiritual dollars.

Today he says I am an idiot who makes no attempt to understand her husband's spiritual work. Today the astral beings are doing a running commentary on all of his actions. Today he is incredible, he has cleansed the sun and the moon, and he is smarter than Albert Einstein and Stephen Hawking.

A year ago he said I was a whore and a slut. A year ago he questioned everything I did, and was suspicious of everything I said. A year ago he relentlessly tormented me with his clairvoyant visions, prevented me from leaving my room, deprived me of sleep, and forced me to perform the sexually perverse acts he was convinced I had committed.

Yesterday I sat beside him in the car while he shouted at our baby for crying. Yesterday he demanded that I yell at her at least half as loud as him because he did not believe I was disciplining her enough. Yesterday my refusal made him furious.

Today I am being punished. Today he keeps me shut inside my room. Today he tells me to think about my disobedience.

Last night I felt something. It felt like something new but also like something from a long time ago that I had forgotten. It felt like the possibility of a different future, being on the cusp of things, the mother bear instinct taking over, my milk letting down for the entire world, I was reborn, everyone was reborn, little babies wanting to be loved, transformation, adventure, running full-speed, headlong into the dark, seeing nothing, nothing, nothing then something, seeing light, mountains and then valleys, valleys and then mountains, I was the hero of my own story, bringing back the boon, love was a madman, my arrow on target, a spinning coin, a planet, teetering and swaying, a widening arc, sorrow was released, travelling long distances, soft fire, death was nothing to fear, swallowing the sea, pouring out of a bucket, a dream, blinking slowly, I was being flayed alive, hurtling towards the horizon, tasting atmosphere, openness, losing my sentimentality, a mission, dangling by a thread, survival, I was so strong, aching, marrow, breath, the strangest feeling, destiny, a burning in my throat, lightning, goodbye, goodbye, goodbye, signs were everywhere, I was bleeding, courage, sweetness and then suffering, suffering and then sweetness, my body floating like seaweed, frogs rejoicing, standing on the precipice, peeling back layers, I was the dear one coming home, circling, circling, then landing, obliteration into love, the only thing left, the only thing I needed to do.

Last night I dreamt of escape.

Today I run.

January 21, 2005

Emergency Safety Plan for Leah Murray and Baby

Leah Murray will be leaving Woodgreen Red Door Shelter when her mother picks her up. Her mother will drive her to Interval House in Kingston where a bed is waiting.
Leah and baby will stay at this shelter for as long as is necessary to ensure her and the baby's safety from Tony Rosato.
Leah will do everything in her power to keep herself and the child safe and will not have any contact with Tony Rosato.

Elisabeth Fitzgerald
CAS Worker

Being little, and living on a northern, golden spruced archipelago, the islands on the boundary between the worlds, in a village so small, I go to the only school there, mixing kids like me, from the temporary military families, with the Native kids whose families had survived the smallpox epidemic of the 1800s and lived there since the beginning.

Shy and mostly keeping to myself, I play with no friends at recess, but stand solitary, holding my limbs stiff and compact in hopes of shrinking into something two-dimensional, a cardboard cut-out, squinting into patches of brisk sunlight, slowly chewing tiny pieces of rice crispy square. I speak infrequently, and when I do, it is a whisper, and only to the comfortingly mysterious ones, like Veronica, the girl whose cheeks are so fat you cannot see her eyes, or Oscar, the boy with no fingernails. And never to the ones like Darla, who is from the very poorest Native family, who wears a dirty yellow dress and dirty runners that are too big, who smells like pee, and smokes cigarettes, and washes her hair in puddles, and beats kids like me to smithereens for looking at her sideways.

On school nights, lying in bed and feeling sick to my stomach, wishing and wishing it could always be Friday night, and still being young enough then to believe, I squeeze my eyes shut tight and hold my breath and wish very hard and over and over again and feel that it just might come true if I am lucky. But all that ever happens is a headful of falling-into-spaghetti dreams of nearly being eaten by giants, and slipping and twirling like a leaf down rain gutter rivers and waterslide sewer pipes, and balancing unnoticed on skyscraper window ledges, peering in through cheek-smudged glass, and becoming suddenly voiceless and breathless and puffed away like a crumpled bit of paper in the wind.

*

Being haunted by magic, and living briefly in a big city with my baby and her father, a man being rapid fire machine-gunned into madness, I peer out from behind furniture into no man's land only during the sparsest moments of eerie calm, and keep my mouth shut.

Helpless and trying to keep invisible, I become less a woman and more like a child shivering under the bed, eye level to the Bogeyman's ankles. And despite being Italian, he calls on his "real ancestors," he says, his Native spirit guides, the eagle and the wolf, to help him wage spiritual warfare against me and my evil demons. The violence lessening when I stop defending myself, I give in to whatever it is he wants me to go along with, give up my own words and echo his: that he has been specially appointed by God to save the planet, and that I am the filthy whore, the stain on his otherwise perfect light. Wearing his own hair and fingernail clippings in a pouch around his neck, a sacred medicine bundle, "to trick them," he says, to fool the demons into attacking *it* instead of *him*, he is happy when I willingly surrender my clothing to him so he can burn it in a smudging ceremony, another temporary fix, just one more in an endless stream of useless offerings and appeasements.

And finally making it still alive to my last night in that sage-smoke-filled apartment, too long tired of crying and wishing and praying, and down to my last set of clothes, I run away with nothing else but my baby to an emergency shelter and sleep and sleep and sleep suddenly and deeply there. Unvigilant at last, though still fretful of that hungry ghost, hovering and buzzing by my pillow, sussing out my softest inside ear, seducing me into the sea, and dreaming me as a suicidal sunken thing, I drift and dally with underwater currents until getting caught up in the net of a fishing trawler, and carried to the sand by fishermen, who comb plankton out of my wet hair, and array the strands like spokes splaying outward from the centre, like sunbeams catapulting from the sun. And then waking within the dream refreshed, still in that lovely amnesia of the split-second of coming-to, before yesterday's sad fingers spider up into the brain, I feel the warm wind on my face like soft daggers reminding me, reminding me.

*

Being on the outskirts in a lonely way, and living alone with my child in the dull safety of a lakeside limestone town, I traipse the ridges and overhangs of unconventional motherhood, a stranger in a strange land, but tinged with my own xenophobia for suburban moms lousy with real wet-eyed pity for me, who talk of nothing but their trusty guppy of a husband's job, or their brand new minivan with all that extra space for new furniture and more diapers, because they are already trying for baby number two.

Stumbling in on things, I am invited to the Native Friendship Centre to learn holistic approaches to motherhood, and I find pregnant girls there like frayed string, bent on trading in their elastic skin for papery thinness and pockmarks, squandering the beautiful tensile stretch of vocal cords on gravel and slackness, cigarettes and crystal meth, losing their kids to the Children's Aid Society, and chuckling out sentences like: "I'm half black and half Blackfoot," and, "Jesus, I can barely sit for getting fucked so hard in the bathroom at the bar last night." And then later, in a tiny closed room, politely being asked to remove my gold jewellery as a sign of solemn respect, I avert my gaze from the elders, all of them so small and crinkled and round, swollen faces and ankles brought on by diabetes and years of hard living, and I listen to their softest, saddest sounds telling residential school survivor stories, and asking how to fill out the claims forms. Barely breathing, yearning to be swallowed whole by a sudden crack in the earth, to disintegrate into one sweet bite of a cyanide tablet, I tuck up into the farthest corner of my brain like a stowaway risking life and limb inside the landing gear compartment of the first plane going anywhere but here.

And that night, on the feathered fringe between sleeping and hallucination, I dream I am wandering a subway tunnel, my baby on my back, looking and looking for the exit but never finding, then arriving at a deserted underground staircase covered in the lost and discarded items of transients and travellers. Coins, small keepsakes, souvenirs, cameras and film, rolls and rolls of used film, all littering the steps, irresistible. Struck with urgency and a feeling of getting away with something, filling my pockets with as much as I can carry, until my clothes might burst, the last thing I take is a tiny stringed instrument, someone's forgotten memento from a trip to Russia. And then while absconding, thinking about all those undeveloped vacations and weddings and birthday parties, I hear plucking sounds, the balalaika playing songs from inside my pocket. It's just the jumbled up effect of something rubbing against the strings as I run, but it feels like music.

Fourteen

the call to adventure: aeroplane

1.
cold lake

alberta,
like a first-time
voodoo pilot,
(woken by dim lit
winter sky)
who plans turns by green
trees, by houses and the marine
set apart from the empyrean.
altimeters aside, he leans
level with his eye on
      the horizon.
but today
is crumbled grey and white
clouds and ice
and he flies
straight down into
      the frozen.

2.
kitty hawk

north carolina,
like a wishful
man initiated on
print and
      bicycles
longs to scythe

        magical
through molecules
lighter than shape,
one day gazes into
god's cold face
        but still
        sun-filled,
he bends wing
and makes
a leap outside of the wind
        tunnel.

AUGUST 10, 2005

BAIL HEARING

BEFORE HER WORSHIP JUSTICE OF THE PEACE C. E. HICKLING

EXAMINATION-IN-CHIEF BY MS. CHRISTIE

MS. CHRISTIE: Just to be clear, Officer McCarthy, what you are about to read is essentially self-reporting by the accused to the police.

DIANE MCCARTHY: That's correct. This is a statement of Detective Sergeant Robert Ritchie, badge number 92. "On March 9, 2005, Tony Rosato advised me of his concerns with respect to his wife and child. He had attended family court in Kingston on March 8, 2005 and observed a woman who looked similar to his wife and presented herself as his wife in court, but definitely was not his wife. Mr. Rosato has a theory that his wife has been involved in a cult – Jehovah's Witnesses. He had noticed in his apartment that many of his wife's belongings, such as clothing, had been switched. He believes the Jehovah's Witnesses have taken his wife and brainwashed her. He also said that prior to his marriage being dissolved, he and his wife had a church wedding, and while he was busy in the kitchen looking after the food for the reception, a female actor who looks similar to his wife posed for pictures. He believes the Jehovah's Witnesses may have been responsible for substituting his wife on this occasion.

"The last time he saw his wife was January 17, 2005. He was told she went to Kingston. He believes she could be at a cottage in Gananoque or in Nevada or Los Angeles or Detroit. Mr. Rosato couldn't elaborate why she would be in these locations other than a hunch. He would appreciate if the border points could be checked to see if she has entered the United States. Mr. Rosato wants verification that his wife and child are all right. He would like the investigator to ensure his wife's identity. She has a reddish birthmark on the left side of her upper lip and extensive dental work in her bottom front teeth. She has very small hands. Mr. Rosato was advised a missing person report would be filed and an investigator would be contacting him. I later learned Detective Constable Jeff Smith was assigned this missing person case."

MS. CHRISTIE: If I could take you to the statement of Officer Jeff Smith.

DIANE MCCARTHY: I'm reading from a statement indicated as that from Detective Constable Jeff Smith, badge number 176. "I received a missing person report on March 10, 2005. Mr. Rosato believes his wife is with her parents and is being held against her will. He was suspicious of the woman who was living with him prior to leaving, and thought she was in fact a different woman, an impostor who had been substituted by Jehovah's Witnesses. Mr. Rosato provided an array of pictures for myself to inspect, noting extremely minor and insignificant differences in exposure and views of his wife, and alleged this to be proof she was a different person than the person he married. Some of these photographs were at a wedding reception and obviously only minutes apart from each other. I informed him that we had been in touch with his wife's legal counsel, Ms. Tina Tom, that there was no concern for Leah's wellbeing, and that she did not want any contact with him. I informed him he could not continue to utilize the police services as a searching mechanism to locate his wife. And if he continued, he could be charged with public mischief. He was understanding and apologized profusely for wasting the police department's resources. This concluded the missing person investigation.

"However, Mr. Rosato contacted me on April 18, 2005, at which time he indicated some extreme concerns about his court-scheduled child visitation on April 15, 2005. He noted he attended the Children's Aid Society in Kingston and was met by Cindy Fitzpatrick. She had arranged for him to have a visitation with his daughter; however, she presented him with a completely different baby. He stated it was necessary for the police to investigate.

"On April 20, 2005, Leah Murray attended an interview during which she elaborated on her life with her husband after they were married, how he was obsessed with evil spirits and all manner of spiritual warfare to the extent that she thought he was harmful to her child's physical welfare, and very detrimental to her own mental and physical health. She explained how she had left the household with her child and a bare minimum of belongings due to her fear. And if Mr. Rosato caught her, there would be no telling how much danger he could be to her. She wished the police to charge her husband for harassment, and hoped to assist in getting him help from mental health facilities.

"Mr. Rosato has since sent an audiocassette of his appointment with a psychic channeller, referencing his vision of the corruption and sexually deviant behaviour of his wife in her past and during their marriage. And most recently, he has sent a package of photographs of his wife and child that he notes are those of the impostor woman and child. I believe Mr. Rosato has the ability to become a danger to his wife and child as he currently reports these persons as impostors. The continued use of police resources to investigate the string of suspicions being reported by the accused, along with the totally irregular types of proof being provided by the accused, make the domestic situation that much more disturbing. I believe the accused, Tony Rosato, has a definite separation from reality."

MS. CHRISTIE: Thank you. Finally, I would like to refer you to a memo from the Children's Aid Society. The author is Cindy Fitzpatrick.

DIANE MCCARTHY: "Tony Rosato attended the agency for a supervised visit with his daughter on April 15, 2005. I took the baby from Leah. The baby was calm as I took her into the access room, but the second she saw Tony she began screaming. I gave her to Tony and he tried to soothe her, but she would not stop crying and screaming. I then tried to calm her and she settled a bit but was very uneasy. Tony saw her two bottom teeth coming in and commented his child was only eight weeks old and could not have teeth coming in already. He stated this was not his child. At this point, I brought the baby back to Leah, where she immediately calmed down. I then returned to speak with Tony. I asked when the baby's birthday was and he said September 26. I asked how she could only be eight weeks old if she was born in September? I then returned to get the baby from Leah. The baby started to cry when I picked her up. I brought her to Tony and she cried even harder. When he was holding her and trying to soothe her, she would not let me out of her sight. She followed me with her eyes every time he moved. Tony handed her back to me saying she was not his child."

MS. CHRISTIE: Thank you. The next Crown witness is Dr. Scott, who is the attending psychiatrist.

JUSTICE OF THE PEACE HICKLING: Dr. Scott, would you please come up here, sir.

MS. CHRISTIE: Your Worship, the Crown would like to qualify Dr. Scott as an expert in the area of psychiatry with training and experience in forensics.

EXHIBIT NUMBER ONE: Curriculum Vitae of Dr. Duncan Scott.
EXHIBIT NUMBER TWO: Dr. Scott's report, dated July 19, 2005, regarding Mr. Rosato.

MS. CHRISTIE: What is your psychiatric diagnosis of Mr. Rosato?

DR. SCOTT: Paranoid schizophrenia.

Q. In addition, is there a particular syndrome that Mr. Rosato suffers from?

A. There's a uniqueness to the presentation of his delusions, what has been named Capgras Syndrome, the feeling that somebody close to you has been duplicated.

Q. Can you characterize that syndrome more fully? It is a misidentification syndrome?

A. That's right. Capgras was first reported in 1923. The opposite of Capgras is Fregoli's Syndrome. And if you know *déjà vu*, that's what happens with Fregoli. Everybody's familiar. They say, "You're my best friend." And Capgras is *jamais vu*. They say, "I've never seen you," to the people they're close to. They don't recognize them whatsoever. In fact, in 1956 the movie *Invasion of the Body Snatchers* was based on this syndrome.

Q. So would it be fair to say that the person who is familiar to the individual suffering from Capgras is seen as an impostor?

A. Yes. Or a duplicate. *L'illusion des sosies.* The illusion of the doubles.

Q. How long was your assessment of Mr. Rosato?

A. It was sixty days. We were quite hopeful that Mr. Rosato would start to gain some insight into the illness and perhaps allow us to investigate further. We tried to help him understand the illness, because the more he understands about it, the less dangerous, perhaps, this could be. But presently, we're really blocked. He refuses any intervention. He has no insight and he won't take any medication. That makes us all very hesitant about this man being at large.

Q. With respect to risk, which is what this bail hearing is about, how does a diagnosis of paranoid schizophrenia with Capgras Syndrome bear on the risk of violence?

A. Both Artuo Silva and Dominique Bourget have done most of the work with this. In the forensic system we find that people who suffer from delusions have a ten-times greater incidence of getting into a violent offence. Ten times more than the average mentally ill individual. And for those suffering from Capgras Syndrome, it's much higher than ten times.

Q. Can you comment on the demographic and clinical features that are important in the progression of Capgras to violence?

A. It's one of emotional worry, and when you speak to Mr. Rosato, there's a very sincere worry that his wife and child have been abducted. And when that starts to combine with the other thoughts he has about being a guardian of light, and his superiority within the universe, there's a huge component of fear he may interfere with the person he thinks is the duplicate. In one case, a son cut off his parents' heads and was looking through their brains trying to find microchips, because he felt they were duplicates. Most recently, last week, in our Brampton court, Dr. Steven Hucker, forensic psychiatrist and colleague, testified to that incident.

<u>EXHIBIT NUMBER THREE</u>: Photocopy of newspaper article.

Q. This is the article you're referring to? The son who is psychotic? Who killed his parents?

A. Yes. He bludgeoned them. First he killed his father in the basement, and then waited for his mother to come down, and then viciously attacked her.

Q. And did he believe his parents were impostors?

A. Yes.

Q. Is there any sexual preoccupation with the progression of violence in Capgras? Are there any other factors?

A. There is some preoccupation with sexual abuse. There is also the presence of auditory hallucinations.

Q. Are those present with Mr. Rosato?

A. Yes, he has auditory hallucinations of the commanding nature. He also displays sexual preoccupation, holding beliefs of past sexual abuse – he thinks his wife was a participant in multiple orgies and incestuous behaviour. And Bourget explains that Capgras sufferers with such sexual preoccupations are even further heightened to violence. Ms. Murray had enough foresight to get out of the household at the time when the behaviour was really manifesting itself at its height. So I think through her own intervention for herself, she may have saved her life.

Q. Is the violence exhibited by individuals who suffer from Capgras impulsive? Or is it planned and deliberate?

A. It's usually predetermined and planned.

Q. I take it there are many more case studies of individuals with Capgras who have attempted to eliminate the impostor and thereby commit homicide of family members.

A. There are many, many cases.

Q. In terms of treatment for individuals who suffer from this mental disorder, does it exist?

A. Yes. Anti-psychotics, usually Risperidone or Olanzapine. In fact, all of Dr. Bourget's cases resolved with the use of Olanzapine.

Q. Has Mr. Rosato been offered a course of treatment?

A. Yes, but he refuses it. He does not believe his illness exists. He believes he's here on trumped up charges. He believes his EEG abnormalities aren't true. He doesn't believe he suffers from Capgras Syndrome, doesn't believe he has any other mental illnesses. He has absolutely no insight into the disorder.

Q. What is your opinion of Mr. Rosato's level of dangerousness?

A. I'm quite concerned. With all the research I've done in all peer review texts, the family members – the doubles – are the ones who are at an extreme level of danger. It's not in any other area. It's not the person just walking by. It's the duplicates. And in this case, it's his wife and child.

the
one
you
love

*

the
one
you
don't

Fifteen

April 19, 2006

HER MAJESTY THE QUEEN V. ANTONIO ROSATO

CHARGE: Criminal Harassment

PROCEEDINGS AT ASSIGNMENT COURT

BEFORE THE HONOURABLE MADAM JUSTICE H. K. MACLEOD

<u>**APPEARANCES**</u>

Ms. P. Christie – Counsel for the Crown

Ms. F. Hawthorn – Counsel for the Accused

MS. HAWTHORN: If I could make a few comments before Mr. Rosato is brought in, which I know is not really appropriate, but I haven't had an opportunity to tell Mr. Rosato that I won't be able to continue to represent him. So I just don't want to say it in open court and shock him. And I don't know who's going to agree to represent him, quite frankly. I can't find counsel willing to take him on.

JUDGE MACLEOD: How long has he been in custody?

MS. CHRISTIE: I think he's been in custody for a year, Your Honour.

JUDGE MACLEOD: Oh my goodness.

MS. CHRISTIE: He's a very difficult individual, Your Honour. He's fired a number of counsel.

JUDGE MACLEOD: Oh my goodness.

MS. CHRISTIE: From the history of Rosato, he's not willing to plead guilty. He wants a trial, but he's basically hurt himself throughout this whole process by just filing, filing, filing, and not communicating with counsel.

JUDGE MACLEOD: Well, let's bring him in and see what we can do.

COURT REPORTER'S NOTE: Mr. Rosato is brought into the courtroom.

MS. HAWTHORN: Your Honour, Mr. Rosato is requesting to speak to you directly.

JUDGE MACLEOD: Yes, Mr. Rosato.

THE ACCUSED: Your Honour, thank you for allowing me to speak. May I ask one thing?

JUDGE MACLEOD: I do not give legal advice, Mr. Rosato. I am a judge. I am not a lawyer.

MR. ROSATO: Can I just ask you about judging?

JUDGE MACLEOD: Yes.

MR. ROSATO: I've been here for eleven months without bail. I feel there's so much corruption around this charge that I really wish for a grand jury investigation of my charge.

JUDGE MACLEOD: We are not in the United States of America. We do not have grand juries, sir, so that is not going to happen, okay?

MR. ROSATO: Thank you, Your Honour.

COURT ADJOURNS

List of Lawyers in Order of Appearance

Richard Bourdeau
is fired because he tells Tony
he primarily practices family law, not criminal.

Murray Rielly
is fired because he admits to Tony
he does not know the Charter of Rights by rote.

Sean Ellacot
is fired because he tries to discuss with Tony
the subject of mental illness.

Felicity Hawthorn
is unable to continue to represent Tony
because she accepts a position as a crown attorney elsewhere.

Craig Mundy
is fired because he tries to discuss with Tony
the subject of mental illness.

Mary Jane Kingston
removes herself from the record because she is accused by Tony
of no longer acting in his best interest.

Chip O'Connor
is fired because he tries to discuss with Tony
the subject of mental illness.

Daniel Brodsky
is appointed by the judge on behalf of Tony
so his case can finally proceed to trial.

August 3, 2006

HER MAJESTY THE QUEEN V. ANTONIO ROSATO

CHARGE: Criminal Harassment

MOTION

BEFORE THE HONOURABLE MR. JUSTICE P. LALONDE

<u>**APPEARANCES**</u>

Ms. P. Christie – Counsel for the Crown

Ms. M.J. Kingston – Counsel for the Accused

MS. KINGSTON: Your Honour, I filed a motion to remove myself from the record on the grounds there is a breakdown in the solicitor and client relationship.

MR. ROSATO: Which I dispute.

MS. KINGSTON: On July 14, Mr. Rosato and I had been working to prepare for his case and he communicated to me that he believed I was no longer acting in his best interest. That concerned me. And the following week, I received a phone call from a staff member at the Quinte Regional Detention Centre. He had received a note from Mr. Rosato expressing that he had lost faith in me as his legal representative.

MR. ROSATO: Your Honour, it only came to my attention a couple of days ago that my lawyer would no longer be representing me.

JUDGE LALONDE: It is not our fault, Mr. Rosato, if you spooked your counsel. She has other things to do besides filing affidavits saying she no longer wants to represent you. What did you say to her that caused her to do that? I am not supposed to know it, but you know what you said to this lawyer. This lawyer has a good reputation and we don't deal with this matter lightly because, especially, you have been in custody now for over a year on this charge.

MR. ROSATO: Seventeen months.

JUDGE LALONDE: But if you doubted the advice she gave to you, then she has no alternative but to bow out.

MR. ROSATO: Thank you, Your Honour. If I may just give my rebuttal. My concerns were for the corruption around the case and the unconscionably long period of time of being incarcerated without bail. I said to her, "Would you please file for coercion, subterfuge and corruption against the case, and against those involved, especially based on the fact that those instigating the charge against me have gone out of their way to keep me in jail for a long period of time."
Quite honestly, it was the Quinte Detention staff. They said, "You know, you should really look at your lawyer. She's the one who's not giving you the straight goods."
I said, "Well, I really trust my lawyer." But are you people honouring the Charter of Rights? I'm not making any allegations. I'm just suggesting that might be the case. So I have filed a lawsuit to question the validity and the corruption in this case. Forgive me if I've gone on too long, Your Honour.

JUDGE LALONDE: I grant Ms. Kingston's application, and her name is to be removed from the record as solicitor for the accused immediately.

MR. ROSATO: Your Honour…

JUDGE LALONDE: I just have to tell you that everything you are saying to me, Mr. Rosato, is carefully recorded here. And it may be used for many issues. And one of the issues I am looking at, and I am going to tell you square in your face, is your mental health issue. This business you went on about corruption here and corruption there, I don't believe any of that. I must tell you that right off the bat.

MR. ROSATO: Well, sir, with all due respect, I consider this to be a mistrial and I ask you to step down from the bench.

JUDGE LALONDE: Well, I haven't started the trial. I'm just talking about your ability to understand the proceedings here. The fact that you think you haven't come to trial yet because of corruption raises some questions.

MR. ROSATO: Well, my mental health is fine. I am an honoured citizen of Canada. I am actually a national monument in this country, sir, and therefore should be accorded the Charter of Rights and Freedoms. I am on the Walk of Fame. And for thirty years now, I've been one of the most outstanding citizens of this country. Mental health has never been an issue in this charge. And under the Charter of Rights, I say this is corruption; it is coercion; it is subterfuge. I say…

JUDGE LALONDE: Please…

MR. ROSATO: May I just finish, please. I am…

JUDGE LALONDE: No, no, no, no, I direct the courtroom. I keep control.

MR. ROSATO: Yes, sir. Forgive me.

JUDGE LALONDE: I want one person to talk at one time, but it doesn't mean I have to sit here and listen to your crap about corruption.

MR. ROSATO: Sir, I...

JUDGE LALONDE: I told you to use another word. Use something else.

MR. ROSATO: Well, sir, I was just quoting...

JUDGE LALONDE: But stop that corruption shit!

MR. ROSATO: I was quoting the Criminal Code. It says coercion and subterfuge. It's in there.

JUDGE LALONDE: But that is not what you said. You said corruption.

MR. ROSATO: Well, that's what coercion and subterfuge are, sir.

JUDGE LALONDE: Well, sorry, sir. Would you sit down, please? Have a seat.

MR. ROSATO: Sir, I am asking you to step down. This is a corrupt case.

JUDGE LALONDE: I am not stepping down. You are wasting your time. Hold your breath.

MR. ROSATO: This is a mistrial.

JUDGE LALONDE: Hold your breath.

MR. ROSATO: Sir, this is a mistrial to me. You are just trying to put me in jail and charge me no matter what. Forgive me.

JUDGE LALONDE: You know the proceedings can go on without you in the courtroom, do you sir? Madam Crown, would you let me know what you intend to do today?

MS. CHRISTIE: Well, your Honour, given the developments here this morning, I'm wondering whether this may be the time for the Court to consider whether or not another mental health assessment may be appropriate.

MR. ROSATO: Just shoot me here, please. I am obviously being held hostage by this judge. If you are going to continuously call mental health every time somebody speaks up for justice, why don't you just step down off that bench here and now, sir?

JUDGE LALONDE: Would you remove this man from my courtroom, please?

MR. ROSATO: I am a member of the Liberal Party. This corruption goes all the way to the top, to the Prime Minister, and I won't stand for it!

COURT REPORTER'S NOTE: Mr. Rosato is removed from the courtroom.

MS. CHRISTIE: Your Honour, there was an assessment almost a year ago that found the accused fit to stand trial, and, in the psychiatrist's opinion, he was NCR (Not Criminally Responsible) at the time of the offence. So we proceeded to set trial dates, but he keeps firing his counsel.

Without a more recent assessment, we run the risk of having yet another counsel appointed who won't be able to take proper instructions, and this accused will stay in the prison system without getting access to treatment. It has already been a year. It's by his own actions that this is happening, but, on the other hand, he is suffering from a mental disorder. So I would encourage Your Honour to consider a motion to order another assessment under the Criminal Code on the issue of fitness to stand trial.

JUDGE LALONDE: As a matter of fact, the reason why I got him to speak so much on the record was to find out, to make up my own mind, as to whether or not this man has mental problems or not. And from all he said to me, and from his outbursts, I'm led to believe that yes, there are mental problems in that man. I'm ordering another sixty-day assessment. And he will be required to be in custody because he is a very dangerous person.

COURT ADJOURNS

Sixteen

Shams of Tabriz

Suntanned, sunflower
-faced, so lit me with glances,
I fell to the ground.

> Layers of my skin
> flamed and peeled off; face, forehead,
> eyelids, like wet lace.

Then gave me water:
the burn victim falls in love
with her rescuer.

> Despite igniting
> me in the first place, for that
> was the greater gift.

September 4, 2007

HER MAJESTY THE QUEEN V. ANTONIO ROSATO

CHARGE: Criminal Harassment

PROCEEDINGS AT TRIAL

BEFORE THE HONOURABLE MR. JUSTICE G. THOMSON

COURT REGISTRAR: Antonio Rosato stands charged that he did harass and without lawful authority engage in threatening conduct directed at Leah Murray or any member of her family thereby causing Leah Murray to reasonably in all the circumstances fear for her safety or for the safety of anyone known to her, contrary to Section 264 (1) (2) (d) of the Criminal Code of Canada. On this indictment how do you plead, guilty or not guilty?

MR. ROSATO: I plead not guilty.

JUDGE THOMSON: Are you ready for your trial, Mr. Rosato?

MR. ROSATO: Yes.

<u>EXAMINATION IN-CHIEF BY MR. BRODSKY</u>

MR. BRODSKY: I understand there's something you wanted to tell His Honour today about your side of the case.

MR. ROSATO: My wife and I never argued once or had any kind of a fight in our home, or anywhere for that matter.

*

Timeline of the Stars and Love and Disaster Begins

13.7 billion years ago
The universe begins.

> Before you there was nothing
> no where, no when
> and now you come at me
> from every corner of the sky
> your mouth like uncoiled heat

13.2 billion years ago
Stars and galaxies form.

> and you are everything
> you are hard and molten and dust
> you are the star and the exploded star

5 billion years ago
The sun is born.

> you are the one who turns the sky red
> who blasts it with fire
> you are the one who boils the oceans

3.8 billion years ago
Earliest life forms appear.

> your spark brings me
> non-living into living
> and I find myself:
> amino acid, protein

700 million years ago
Primitive animals appear.

> breathing now
> I inhale raindrops
> as big as apples
> or giant ocean pearls

200 million years ago
Mammals evolve.

> and I find myself:
> bone, hair, and skin

600,000 years ago
Homo sapiens evolve.

> being born now
> I lose my fetal gill slits
> and take that first breath
> oxygen ripping through
> my unmapped lungs.

*

MR. ROSATO: After my wife and daughter disappeared, the police department filed a missing person report. They assured me she was at a shelter, and about a week later I was notified of custody proceedings, never having had any prior notice whatsoever. Under marital law in this country and in any democracy, if your wife with a baby is planning to leave your home under duress, the husband is supposed to receive prior notice. She must say to you, "Husband, under for better or for worse, through sickness, through health, I'm about to leave, and this is why." That didn't happen, so I was very concerned for her whereabouts.

Oh and by the way, in our first Family Court proceeding, I was very alarmed that my wife was not present. There was another girl sitting next to my wife's lawyer, Tina Tom. So I told this to my lawyer, Richard Bourdeau, and he said, "Don't make any comment about it right now." And I said, "Well, I have a photograph of myself and my wife in our marriage. And that's not my wife."

So after the proceeding, I left and went to the Toronto Police Department. I spoke to them about it. I said, "Excuse me, but I was just in a custody proceeding where we're deliberating the custody of my baby, and my wife wasn't present. Is that customary? I mean, isn't that somewhat, you know, insensitive?"

They said, "Well, Mr. Rosato, seeing that you're a celebrity, it happens all the time. Many people don't want to show up in the courtroom for fear of the paparazzi." And that's, I'm sure, what happened.

I went to another Family Court proceeding. My wife was there. She did not look well. She was being chaperoned by a stranger, someone I didn't recognize.

And then I went to my first supervised visitation with my daughter and they brought her in bleeding! She was bleeding from the nose profusely. Her face was swelled up. He nose was caved in to one side, recovering from somebody punching her, and her lip was healing from what I considered to be a cut. I could tell from the appearance of her skin that somebody was anxious to get her healed quickly for the visitation. She looked like she was weathering some sort of antibiotic, maybe even Cortisone, and I was very, very frightened for what had happened to my daughter.

Then, when I had my second supervised visit, they handed me another baby, who was not my daughter, and I immediately felt very terrified. I said, "Excuse me, but this is not my daughter." They said, "Well, are you sure, Mr. Rosato?"

I said, "Yes."

From that point on I was very concerned, as one would imagine, about what was going on. I had not heard from my wife and daughter, although her lawyer had contacted my lawyer. But I was also very concerned about my wife's lawyer, Tina Tom. Tina Tom is obviously a, you know, an admitted lesbian, which I felt is not an issue for my wife to be dealing with. My wife spoke very vehemently against parents who participate in and perpetuate bisexuality in their home to justify incest with their children. I found it rather unconscionable.

*

December 26, 1954

Tony is born in Fontanarosa, Italy, to Raphael and Maria Rosato.

1958

Tony travels by boat to Canada with his mother and father.

1961

Raphael returns to Italy for epilepsy treatment.
Tony grows up in Ottawa. He loves comic books and imagines himself as a superhero. His mother works long hours as a seamstress at the London Fog coat company and often leaves him in the care of a Jewish family.

1966

Tony and his mother receive the news that Raphael has died.

December 17, 1976

I am born in Chilliwack, British Columbia, to David and Connie Murray.

1979

Tony moves to Toronto and starts doing improv at The Second City.

1980

Tony joins the cast of SCTV and works alongside John Candy, Eugene Levy, Andrea Martin, Joe Flaherty, Dave Thomas, Rick Moranis, and Catherine O'Hara. He creates his most well known character, Marcello Sebastiani.

*

MR. ROSATO: When my wife was pregnant, we were thinking of having our baby at the Kingston General Hospital. There was an obstetrician named Dr. Hately who was going to attend to our birth. I decided not to have Dr. Hately because, as she was examining my wife, she put her hands on my wife's womb and said, "Would you like me to take a guess using my hands as to whether you have a boy or girl?"

I said, "How do you plan to do that?" Because I'm sure she meant actually trying to use some sort of spiritual magic, since she clearly wasn't talking about any technical observation. I have been a spiritual worker for most of my life, and actually a rather profound one in the sense that I've done a lot of work in researching it, and I didn't appreciate her Wiccan approach. Witchcraft, by the way, is the manipulation of the living force. Everyone knows that the planet is alive. The planet is spinning around the sun every day – call it software, call it sacred intelligence – it's the same software that's underneath our feet and, therefore, part of our own intelligence, and it is sacred. Everyone that has a child knows you can't manipulate it through spells.

So with that having been said, I found it very frightening that Dr. Hately was venturing into all that. I also thought it alarming that she was a complete dead ringer, a duplicate – and judging by these proceedings I know this may sound a little, you know, odious, but regardless – she had a frightening resemblance to Leah's mother.

Now I don't mean that to be a derogatory statement by any means, but I was worried about Leah's family being involved with incest and pedophilia. And then I see my wife is in a medical centre that was suggested to her by her own incestuous father and mother. I said, "Okay. Well, Leah, how did you end up at this medical centre?"

She said, "My father and mother brought me here."

I said, "I see. And they're the ones you're terrified of, the ones who always abuse you, and the doctor looks exactly like your mom. Okay, I can accept that, but I'm going to feel a little bit more comfortable if we have our baby in Toronto."

*

1981–1982

> Tony joins the cast of Saturday Night Live. He gets addicted to cocaine. He is fired.

1985–1989

> Tony gets the role of Arthur "Whitey" Morelli on the Canadian police drama Night Heat.

1987–1989

> Tony plays Lieutenant Lou Gianetti on the Canadian television series Diamonds.

1990–1991

> Tony does the voice for Nintendo's character Luigi on the television show The Adventures of Super Mario Bros. 3 and Super Mario World.

1991-2001

Tony does voice work for numerous animated series and occasionally gets small acting roles.

2001–2003

Tony sells his house in Toronto and moves to Los Angeles in hopes of becoming a star. But he gets few auditions and even less work. He turns his focus to New Age spirituality and learns how to read Tarot cards. He collects dozens of large crystals, to be used for healing, some weighing as much as five pounds. He has a breakdown and keeps himself locked in his apartment, burning incense. He sleeps with a giant wooden cross in his bed. He sees the flames of the Holy Spirit leaping out from behind his shower curtain and he is terrified. He comes back to live with his elderly mother in Toronto.

*

MR. ROSATO: Now going back to the Family Court in Kingston, my wife was there at the second proceeding. She did not look well. She looked clearly controlled by whoever had brought her in. I was very concerned about that. I was not allowed to speak to her. I then went to the Toronto Police Department and voiced my opinions about her medical records and her psychiatric and abuse history.

I was met in my home by a homicide detective. I told him I was very concerned once again about my wife's reckless abandonment. It's not my wife; she wouldn't do that. Somebody had left a computer disc, which I showed to the detective. It was marked "wedding photos." I downloaded the pictures. They were pictures of our wedding. They had been taken by I assume her brother, although I never actually saw him take the pictures. This disc was very troubling to me.

Somebody had digitally manipulated the various photos of our wedding pictures and superimposed other girls in the photos, which I thought was a joke, and a bad one at that, considering the sanctity of wedding pictures. And there was a lot of clothing missing from our home. I went to my wife's closet, which I'm not accustomed to doing. I have never ripped any of my wife's clothing. I've never destroyed anything of my wife's except a couple of things that my wife asked me to destroy.

When my wife and I were cleansing her apartment and moving everything to Toronto, we had to make everything baby friendly. My wife said, "Would you look through all the things in my apartment and discern what's necessary for us to throw out?" We started with a lot of the books on Satanism and witchcraft that her mother and father had given her. We didn't feel it was appropriate.

We threw out mirrors. Mirrors, because a psychiatrist had convinced her it was all right to look at a mirror while you're making love to someone, especially yourself. I found that highly degrading and disgusting. I said, "Who gave you that permission?" We talked about things always with sanctity, democratically, gently, lovingly and caringly. That's how you talk to someone who's been abused and raped throughout her entire life. That's who I am. I'm an actor, but I'm not just an actor. My work, all the things I've done, are shows of conscience, and I challenge anyone to look at that.

So we discussed everything gently. And at one point she said, "You know, my father really likes the idea of these mirrors in here. He gave them to me."

I said, "Okay, and what should we do with them?" Because mirrors, as anyone who's studied mirrors understands, are photographs.

Spiritually, everyone knows what Aboriginal people and all indigenous people feel about mirrors: they capture a little bit of your soul. Why? Because it's the basis of photography, silver nitrate, it's emulsion at the back of a mirror and it receives and retains images. If you're a spiritual worker, one of the first things you do in someone's home is you cleanse their mirrors. Everyone knows that a mirror is sacred. Why? Because it reflects the light of God of your own beingness or higher power, however way you define it.

Mirrors are very sacred and if they're used in some sort of degradation then you don't want them in your home, you just really don't. So we agreed we should throw them out.

She had a group of dolls, which, by the way, I never destroyed, never touched them once in my life. But I looked at them and I said, "Excuse me, where did you get these dolls?" Here's a doll of a Spanish dancer, with her arm lifting her dress up. Here's another one of a milkmaid. Here's another one of a geisha girl. I said, "These are all very strong archetypes for children. They're really not appropriate for a child. Why would you keep a flamenco dancer lifting her dress up, and a milkmaid with a mini-skirt, and a geisha, for a little child?"

She said, "Well, my mom wanted me to have these."

I said, "Okay, well, I don't mind that, but, you know, judging by your incestuous background, and your mother promoting bisexuality to you at all times, are they really appropriate?"

So I found it really inappropriate to provide adult dolls for a baby, but I certainly would never have destroyed them. I left all the decisions to my wife. Even with the mirrors, I said, "Hon, what do you want us to do with these things? It's your decision." I always wanted my wife to feel completely empowered because anybody who's gone through that kind of sexual abuse needs to be empowered at all times in every way, certainly regarding the sanctity of her personal, sacred space.

*

October 2002

SCTV is inducted into Canada's Walk of Fame.

September 4, 2003

Tony and I meet in Toronto. He tells me I have a beautiful light about me. We discover we both have birthdays in December, we both love Rottweilers.

September 5, 2003

I watch him perform as the host for a show in honour of the thirtieth anniversary of The Second City. Excitement sprouts up inside me like a newborn bean.

October 6, 2003

It is our first date. The sun shines on his face. We sit together in a park, and my hand moves in wide arcs across his back. He makes a strange sound in my ear, like a whimper, and we kiss. Nearby, an old woman does Tai Chi.

October 8, 2003

We have our second date in a private karaoke room. He is wearing what he always wears: a white dress shirt, black jeans, and black cowboy boots. I am wearing a black and white dress, black tights, and black boots. He tells me I look like some kind of superhero.

November 28, 2003

We get officially engaged.

December 17, 2003

Tony visits me on my birthday. He has six hundred dollars to spend. We take taxis everywhere. He even asks a taxi driver to wait for him, the meter running, while he goes into stores to buy me presents. He gives

ten dollars at a time to street people. Later that
evening, he gets upset when he thinks I am attracted
to our waitress.

December 31, 2003

We go to Kingston City Hall to get a marriage license.
We fill out the forms and Tony asks the clerk if he can
leave his birth date blank, because he doesn't want me
to know how old he is. "And anyway, I am eternal," he
says.
We take a bus to Toronto and get married at City
Hall.
We return by bus to Kingston that night. It's late, and
we are tired. In the bedroom, Tony demands to know
if I have been faithful to him. "Of course I have," I say.
"I'm not so sure," he says. Then he shuts the door and
interrogates me all night and into the next day, and
will not let me up off the bed until I confess to all his
terrible accusations.

*

MR. ROSATO: With that having been said, her clothing; I
would never touch anyone's clothing. My wife asked me to
make a comment on all the micro mini-skirts that were given
to her by her father and mother. I said, "Why would your father
and mother have you wear micro mini-skirts at twenty-seven
years old when you're an incest victim?" So that was an issue.
I started buying other clothes for my wife, clothes that were
what I considered to be the kinds of clothes she was going to
have to wear for having a baby – dresses that were longer and
would facilitate the growing of her womb. And she was very
happy about that. I never saw those other clothes again. I don't

know what happened to them. That was her responsibility. Every conversation I always had with her was like, "Well, hon, whatever you feel you should do with them, please do, but these are my opinions on it."

I then became aware of all the Internet pornography she had. I said, "You know, you spend an awful lot of time on the Internet. How come you're on the Internet at all times?"

She said, "Well, you know, I'm in the chat rooms."

I said, "Well, who authorized this? Why are you doing this? It doesn't make sense to me that you, having an incestuous history, would participate in this kind of degradation."

She said her psychiatrist had told her to unleash her pent-up sexual frustrations with pornography. Well, I found that to be unconscionable. It's like saying to someone with a heroin addiction problem, "Why don't you do some more heroin?" I think that's just ridiculous, and I think everyone knows you try to keep the degradation level in someone's home and life to the most sacred level possible. You need to release it completely and get rid of any degrading influences whatsoever.

With that having been said, she said most of the material was given to her by her ex-boyfriend. We discussed it. She decided she was going to stop the Internet services, chat rooms and so forth. We both agreed on that. Having a baby coming, we didn't need pornography in our home. This was all part of the cleansing.

She had photos. We tore them up together. Looking back at it, I wish we could have sent them to the police department, but it was my wife's decision. It was her personal property. She wanted to rip them up, so we ripped them up. She asked me to look through all her photo albums and said, "Could you look through all this material and determine for me whether you think there's anything questionable for our baby?" I said I would.

Now my wife told me her father had burst in on her in the bathroom at all times when she was naked up to the age of twelve and snapped photos of her at all times, not just during the bath, but using the bathroom. I found that really horrible. With that having been said, I proceeded to look through the photo album and wondered what I would find there. There were a few pictures taken of her with her childhood friends, which I found, as an intuitive person, to be a little questionable. I said to her, "I find these questionable. What do you want to do with them? Well, if you feel uncomfortable with them, let's rip them up."

There were three pictures, that was it, and we did it, and it was done. We didn't just do these things haphazardly. We talked about things all the time. It was an ongoing conversation.

Someone might say, well, why did you decide to have a child, Mr. Rosato, considering all of that? And to be quite honest with you, clearly anyone would not have planned to have a baby under these circumstances. I want that understood.

Originally, as I became aware of what my wife was going through, it became clear we would not have a baby for a very, very long time. But my wife was terrified about losing me and losing our marriage, and I could see that, and I could see she had been waiting for a very long time for someone to help her get away from her family.

With that having been said, she started to reveal more and more information to me, especially on our wedding night. She conveyed to me she was having a lot of extracurricular sexuality and she was terrified. She wanted to reveal it to me on our wedding night because it was a sacred time to discuss it. But I was very frightened because I could see it was clearly a terrible, terrible abuse issue she was wrestling with.

I don't consider my wife to be schizophrenic in any way. I consider her to be, with all due respect to all the Jewish people who have suffered, I consider her to be a Holocaust victim by virtue of how much suffering she's had to deal with. She is a Jewish girl and I consider her to have suffered very much in that home along with her twin or triplet sisters, or these other duplicate girls that have been talked about.

That summarizes all that happened in my wife's apartment in Kingston. I've tried to bring together here the understanding of what happened in our home, how this hearsay came about, how these allegations came about, what my reactions were to them, and the chronology of these proceedings and how I ended up here.

*

January 31, 2004

I discover I am pregnant.

March 20, 2004

Tony and I get married again, this time in Kingston, at St. Mary's Catholic Church.

April 10, 2004

I am baptized.

July 2004

Tony renounces our faith.

September 2004

Tony moves me to Toronto. We have no money. Tony brings food back from his mother's apartment: celery, tomatoes, grapes, and bread. We go for long walks, and Tony wears holes into the bottoms of his cowboy boots. "I love it when the greats walk down the street," someone says to him as we pass by.

September 26, 2004

Our daughter is born.

December 26, 2004

It is Tony's birthday. Halfway around the world there is an earthquake in the ocean and a tsunami kills thousands and thousands of people in South East Asia. The earth wobbles on its axis. Tony gives over to complete madness.

January 14, 2005

Tony is going on and on about his spirit animals. "I have the wolf on my side," he says. "I have the eagle and the owl and the raven. I have the coyote and the cougar. I have the lion and the elephant and the rhinoceros. I have the porcupine and the scorpion. I even have the praying mantis. It may be small, but after sixteen billion years, its spirit is the size of the solar system." He pauses and looks down at me, seated in the rocking chair, nursing my baby. "You must no longer breastfeed our daughter. Your milk is unclean. After all, they don't let crackwhores breastfeed," he says.

"I'm not a crackwhore," I say.

"Oh, aren't you?"

And suddenly I am overcome by the teeth and the tongue, the thick fur and the claws, and the eyes, the angry, wild eyes of the mother bear growing out of my back.

*

MR. ROSATO: Now later on, when I went to Kingston to speak to Detective Jeff Smith, I was not told whatsoever of any restraining order. Regardless, I had no intention of trying to illegally look for my wife, even though there was no illegality within it, even if I had wanted to. I was there to find out whether I should be worried about someone taking my daughter fraudulently, through extortion.

Detective Jeff Smith did not want to look at the wedding photographs. He kind of glanced at them briefly but made no comment. He said, "Do you love your wife?

I said, "Yes, of course I love my wife."

He said, "Well, then don't worry about it." He shook my hand and that was it.

So there's the custody proceeding where my wife was not in attendance, which was once again my concern. Where was my wife? Why was my wife not in a custody proceeding? There's pornography, there's incest. Can anybody see why I would be concerned about where my wife was and where my daughter was? It's not really that unreasonable to ask under those circumstances, and I wanted someone to investigate why this other girl was there.

Then there's the visitations with my daughter. Detective Jeff Smith contacted me, said, "Mr. Rosato, I have some information about your daughter. Would you like to come into Kingston?"

I said, "Well, actually, having spoken to my Family Court lawyers, Singer and Kwinter, they recommend that I do not."

He said, "I would like you to come in and do a video interview."

I said, "On the suggestion of my lawyers, they highly recommend that I don't." We hung up the phone.

He called me back a few days later and said, "Mr. Rosato, would you like to get some information on your daughter, yes or no?"

I said, "Well, once again I don't think it's appropriate for me to come into Kingston." And at this point I'm beginning to feel like a rather insensitive parent.

Here I am, you know, asking about the whereabouts of my daughter. I have a homicide detective saying, "Would you like to come to Kingston?" What am I going to say, well, you know, let my lawyers handle it? I felt that was inappropriate because he sounded like he really had some strong information about what's going on.

So I went there once again. When I showed up he said, "Mr. Rosato, I would like to sit down and do a video interview with you."

I said, "With all due respect, you told me you had information about my baby and you told me we weren't going to be doing the video."

So he said, "Well, come on downstairs."

I went downstairs and he proceeded to arrest me.

*

January 17, 2005

I escape with my baby. I go to a nearby family shelter where I call my father and tell him I have left Tony. For five nights, I sleep on a cot with my arms wrapped tightly around my baby, next to another homeless woman and her two children. During the days, I cry and tell my story to anyone who will listen. My baby cries from colic. I cry in the bathroom. I cry during mealtimes. I wade through the sea of hours, my eyes stinging from a strange mixture of salt and sadness and relief. I feel nearly blind. Finally, my mother and my aunt come to get us. We drive to Kingston in the worst blizzard my mother has ever seen, but I am oblivious to it.

January 22, 2005

My mother brings my baby and me to Kingston Interval House, a shelter for women and children. And though I am free of Tony, I am not – despite everything, I still care for him. Despite all the terror and abuse he inflicted on me, I want to help him. The counsellors say my feelings are normal.

May 5, 2005

Tony is arrested. He is sent to the psychiatric hospital for an assessment.

July 19, 2005

Dr. Duncan Scott declares Tony fit to stand trial. Tony is given a choice: to wait for his trial in hospital and receive treatment on a voluntary basis, or go untreated and wait for his trial at the Quinte Regional Detention Centre. He chooses prison.

August 10, 2005

Tony has a bail hearing. No one is willing to be his surety, and he is considered too dangerous to be released into his mother's care. Bail is denied.

December 5, 2005

The preliminary inquiry is set to start, but Tony fires his lawyer and is sent back to Quinte.

March 15, 2006

The preliminary inquiry takes place. I am petrified, sitting in the witness box, giving my testimony, Tony just inches away in the defendant's box. A screen has been placed in front of him so I do not have to look at him, do not have to feel his eyes on me. The trial is set for August.

*

MR. BRODSKY: Mr. Rosato, can I just direct your attention to two areas that you were talking about? One, did your wife testify at the preliminary inquiry, and two, did somebody bring another child to the second meeting with the Children's Aid Society?

MR. ROSATO: Your last question first. I have not seen my daughter since the first visitation, and at that time she was clearly abused. The second question, yes, from day one there was more than one Murray girl. There's not just Leah Murray. I contend there's a Leah Murray and a couple of sisters, and I've been asking about that from day one and no one, but no one, will give me any verification of that.

Now I've had two and half years to think about this and decide for myself, you know. Is this extortion and fraud on my wife's part, or is it her family? Was there more than one girl in my home? Is that why they presented this other girl at the Family Court proceeding? Was it to say: "Mr. Rosato, we do things in our own way in this town, and yeah, there was more than one girl in your family and here she is, and you may have had sexual relations with her, so we're presenting her as one of the women in your life, as your wife."

Now I thought, Well, if that's the case, what a disgusting and degrading way to tell someone. Could you not have had one person in this town, some law-abiding citizen with no police record, who sits on Crown property on King Street in some modest way, say: "Mr. Rosato, there may be more than one woman in this family and you may have been deceived in the bedroom?"

And over these past two and a half years I've had a good chance to look at it and I contend that's probably what happened. I make no bones about it. My concern about it is, was it done maliciously? I said…

JUDGE THOMSON: Mr. Rosato, before you go on, I just want to make sure I have a clear note on this. Mr. Brodsky asked you whether or not your wife testified at the preliminary hearing, and you said she did testify. Let us just do that up and then go ahead.

MR. ROSATO: All right. I was concerned about how many girls there were in this family, whether Leah has a twin sister or two twin sisters. The woman that was in the preliminary inquiry, when they brought her in, they had a wig on her head, covering her face entirely. They had a screen in front of my face, under the pretension that my wife was supposedly, allegedly, frightened about speaking to me in the courtroom.

Once again, in judicial law, under the Charter of Rights, under democracy, one is innocent until proven guilty, and has the right to face their accuser. And I was still married so it was already unconscionable to try to pit my wife against me, and drag our marriage through a court proceeding. But nevertheless, they said, "Well, can you recognize that girl over there?"

I said, "Well, there's a screen in front of my face, and there's a wig that's covering her head entirely. If you're asking if I knew there was more than one woman in my marriage, well, that's *your* job to tell *me*."

I came to the homicide department of two different police departments saying, "Excuse me, but is someone extorting me in this marriage? Do I have a reason to be concerned that a helpless, hapless actor is being taken advantage of by twins or triplets who then walk off with a baby to an incestuous family?"

So there I was in the courtroom saying, "Why am I not being allowed to determine whether this is actually my wife or not? It sounds like my wife. Yes, I recognize my wife's voice."

With that having been said, as far as I could tell vocally, yes, it was my wife, but as anybody in any courtroom in any democracy in the world knows, you should have the right to not have a screen in front of your face, or your accuser dressed up in a wig. The question at that time was, well, hey, you know, if *you* can't tell, how am *I* supposed to tell? You're law enforcement officers. You're court officials. That's what *I* came to ask. I want to know whether someone is taking advantage of me. I humbly request and submit, yes, I might be vulnerable to extortion and fraud, if that's what everyone wants to know. And this harassment charge is hearsay. To me it's distortion – libellous, slanderous distortion of conversations that my wife and I had, and many of these allegations are out and out lies.

MR. BRODSKY: Thank you. Your Honour, those are the questions that I have of this witness.

*

May 8, 2006

> I am granted sole custody of my daughter. Tony is not even allowed a supervised visit.

August 2006

> The trial is postponed when Mary Jane Kingston steps down as Tony's lawyer and Tony is ordered back to the psychiatric hospital for another fitness assessment.

October 2006

> Dr. Michael Chan finds Tony fit to stand trial. The trial is set for March 2007.

March 2007

> The trial is postponed and rescheduled for August.

May 2007

> The story becomes national news.

August 2007

Tony's trial commences. A handful of his show business friends make the trek from Toronto to show support. That same day I see Dan Aykroyd lumbering down Princess Street. He tells the newspapers he hopes Tony gets treatment.

I have been warned to stay away from the courthouse during the trial. Most of the Crown's case depends on my very real fear of Tony, which would be put into question if I were to bring myself so close as to be in the same room as him.

But it is very strange to be so sequestered, to wake up every morning and find out about my life from the newspapers. Sometimes there are photos of Tony. He is handcuffed, or holding a folder with the Star of David drawn on it. He looks old and alien to me. His hair is long and thin and tied back.

*

JUDGE THOMSON: Anything else, Mr. Rosato?

MR. ROSATO: Well, I humbly submit to my solicitor, does that answer the question adequately? Because what I'm concerned about is the harassment charge. In order for there to be a charge of harassment, or any charge, you need witnesses, you need evidence. When I was told I was being charged with harassing my wife throughout our entire marriage, I said, "Well, excuse me, but there was nobody in our marriage other than my wife and me. Nobody ever witnessed our marriage regardless of whether or not there was any grounds for these allegations."

There was nobody. Detective Jeff Smith never once entered our home and spoke to us. There were no police department officials ever called to our home to answer any concerns about harassment, never in the whole nine months of expecting our baby, or in the whole three and half months after she was born. There was never any conversation about harassment by anybody. If I had really, truly harassed her throughout our entire marriage, somebody would have certainly heard about it. On the other hand, after my wife and daughter recklessly abandoned our home, I found evidence of a cell phone bill. Her father and mother had delivered a cell phone to her. There were ninety-nine phone calls back to Kingston. Now under marital law, if my wife was sitting there on a cell phone talking to her incestuous parents behind my back, ninety-nine times in a two-month period unbeknownst to me, well, that's an absolute attack on our marriage, and anybody under marital law knows that. It's called an abuse of your marriage.

My wife said to me she did not want her family to even know where we were having our baby. She said, "Please, please don't let them know." Now what's a husband to say?

A husband would say: "Honey, we've got to let your family know. I mean, everybody should know. We should celebrate." But she was in tears. She did not want her father and mother to even know where we lived. I said, "Well, what if there's an emergency? We must at least let them have the phone number so they can call us twenty-four hours of the day."

And if I could make one more statement, when you live with someone who's a victim of pedophilia and incest, then in my home there is no such thing as sexuality. We believe in making love, and we were celibate throughout most of our relationship. When we found out we were having a baby, we were completely celibate and graciously protective of each other's bodies at all times. Those innuendos I was sexually inappropriate with my wife were very, very harmful to our marriage and our relationship because they suggested such desecration and degradation, and I've found that to be one of the most heinous things I've had to deal with in the last two and a half years.

MR. BRODSKY: Your Honour, that's the case for the defence.

JUDGE THOMSON: Okay, thank you. Any reply?

MS. CHRISTIE: No cross-examination.

MR. ROSATO: For the record, Your Honour, I love my wife very, very much, regardless of the confusion with her or her sisters. I forgive her and love her completely.

COURT ADJOURNS

September 5, 2007

HER MAJESTY THE QUEEN V. ANTONIO ROSATO

CHARGE: Criminal Harassment

REASONS FOR SENTENCING

BEFORE THE HONOURABLE MR. JUSTICE G. THOMSON

JUDGE THOMSON: At the commencement of the evidentiary phase I reviewed the letter from Dr. Scott, dated July 19, 2005, where he gave his opinion that Rosato was fit to stand trial.

I have observed Mr. Rosato from the very beginning of this trial and have spoken to him at various times. He understands everything I have said to him. I am satisfied he is capable of understanding the available pleas. He understands the nature and purpose of the proceedings. There is no question in my mind at all that he is able to communicate rationally with his counsel and with me when I've spoken to him. I am satisfied beyond a reasonable doubt that the accused is fit and has been fit throughout to stand trial.

He was clear that he was pleading not guilty and denied all of the allegations made by the complainant and denounced the case against him as libellous, slanderous, dishonest and dishonourable. All in all, it made for a very bizarre hour of evidence.

I cannot accept the evidence of the accused as being credible, believable or reliable in any way, shape or form and, therefore, do not believe it.

I accept the evidence of the complainant as it was fully cross-examined upon and not successfully challenged in any significant way.

Therefore, I am satisfied beyond a reasonable doubt that Antonio Rosato harassed Leah Murray and did engage in threatening conduct directed at Leah Murray or her daughter, thereby causing Leah Murray to reasonably, in all circumstances, fear for her safety or anyone known to her, specifically her daughter.

Did Antonio Rosato know his conduct harassed Leah Murray? There is no question in my mind the complainant's protestations on things like the sexual acts, for example, were known to the accused and he was aware that his conduct harassed the complainant. He was also aware there was a risk that his conduct harassed her, but went ahead anyway, not caring.

Did Antonio Rosato's conduct cause Leah Murray to fear for her own and her daughter's safety, and was her fear reasonable in all circumstances? I am satisfied what he did or said caused her to fear for her and her daughter's safety, and any reasonable person in the same circumstances would fear for their safety.

Therefore, I am satisfied there be a finding of guilt on the charge before the court.

The offender is to reside as a new patient for a period of up to three years at Providence Care Mental Health Services, 752 King Street West, Kingston, Ontario.

MR. ROSATO: Excuse me?

JUDGE THOMSON: Yes, sir?

MR. ROSATO: Is there no consideration at all for the fact that I've spent two and a half years in jail already before the trial?

JUDGE THOMSON: Yes, I think that has been taken into account, Mr. Rosato.

MR. ROSATO: Well, you've just sent me to three years imprisonment in a psychiatric ward.

JUDGE THOMSON: No, sir, I have sent you for three years at the discretion of the Providence Care Mental Health Services to determine when and if during that three-year period you are going to be able to be released into the public domain.

MR. ROSATO: But I have absolutely no record. I'm on the Walk of Fame in front of the Princess of Wales Theatre. I'm an accomplished performer. I have been a citizen of note for the past thirty years. I've never harmed anyone in my life. If I knew there was going to be this kind of heinous treatment by my own wife, I surely would have come in here and said, "Please, Mrs. Rosato, let Leah Ruth Murray come in here and let's talk about this, let's face the trial!"

JUDGE THOMSON: Mr. Rosato, this was a very, very difficult case for everybody involved.

MR. ROSATO: Well, sir, I spent two and a half years in jail and now I'm going to be spending three years in a psychiatric ward for something I didn't do. That's very unfair, Your Honour, very unfair.

JUDGE THOMSON: I hear what you're saying, but I disagree with you.

MR. ROSATO: It's a miscarriage of justice, Your Honour. May I appeal at some point?

JUDGE THOMSON: You can do whatever you want to do after I walk out of this courtroom.

MR. ROSATO: Thank you, Your Honour.

JUDGE THOMSON: Within reason.

COURT ADJOURNS

*

September 5, 2007

Tony is found guilty, but he is not found NCR. It means the hospital where he has been sentenced is still not allowed to force him into treatment. Tony will have to appear before a Consent and Capacity Board first, and be found incapable of making his own treatment decisions. Tony can appeal that finding. And then, after all his appeals are exhausted, a substitute decision-maker must be appointed for him.

May 2008

Tony's illness gets sufficiently bad enough for him to be declared incapable of making his own treatment decisions. Because the trial is over (I am no longer the complainant and he is no longer the accused), and because we are still officially married, I am appointed his substitute decision-maker. It has been over three years since I left Tony, over three years of feeling powerless to get him help. And now the power is in my hands alone. I sign the forms allowing the hospital to force him into treatment immediately. Over the course of the year, Tony's mental health improves, and he gains enough insight to take his medication voluntarily.

December 2008

The hospital determines Tony is no longer a danger to my daughter or me and discharges him. He goes back to live with his mother in her tiny Toronto apartment.

July 15, 2010

I am granted a divorce, the freedom I sought five and a half years ago, finally mine.

Seventeen

On Looking Back:
I can only know how soft my skin is by how hard rocks are

I do such strange things in this place
stranger than the stars
       this one that wavers
       or has wings in the shape of a moth

my mind is elsewhere
       pulling bodies from debris
       waiting for news of the survivors
       I am jealous of the young stars in their dusty cocoons
       formed from what remains
              less life to remember

Mars may have once had oceans
I dived into waterless depressions
       into the crook of his arm, too

the freight of memory suggests
       this fish was a shark

54Black26 wakes up to the sound of tapping. Clear as day, somebody using Morse code. *Where am I? Where am I?* It's 76Red17, the newest arrival. Came in the night before, disoriented from the journey.

54 taps back: *You're at the Epithelial Penal Colony, iron ore mines.* Silence.

Probably needs a minute to assimilate that kind of information, 54 thinks.

In the Golgi Galaxy? 76 taps. *It can't be.*

It's true. 54 taps back. *Meet me at the Nuclear Membrane tomorrow morning, before they send us down.*

*

At the Nuclear Membrane:

"How did I get here?" 76 asks, upset. "The last thing I remember, I was minding my own business crossing the street. I felt something heavy all over my body. And the next thing I know, I'm here."

"Yeah, but you must have done something to get here," 54 says. "Nobody gets here from just minding their own business. I know why I'm here."

"What do you mean?" asks 76.

"I did some very bad things," says 54.

"Oh. Well I didn't do anything bad!"

"Well you must have done *something*, is all I'm saying."

"No! I don't deserve to be here! Maybe I told a few lies, broke a few rules, but I don't deserve this. I'm making a run for it first chance I get!"

"You can't. There are guards all over the perimeter. You don't stand a chance."

A loud bell rings, and the prisoners file onto the massive freight elevator that lowers them into the bowels of the planet.

*

Another morning. 54's cell walls pulse with more Morse code. This time it's 04Green26. Another new arrival, but one who has their wits about them.
I figured it out. I know how to escape.
How? 76, still agitated, jumps in.
We need to work together. That's the only way. If we make a pact to help each other, they let us walk!
I'm in! 76 taps loudly.
Me, too, taps 54.

*

Later, by the Mitochondrial Furnaces:
"76, tell me what you want, and I'll do it," says 54.
"I need to learn patience. I need to stop being so scared of things. I want to face challenges and learn forgiveness," says 76.
"Okay, I can help you with that," says 54. "But I'll have to hurt you, and you won't remember this agreement we made right here and now. Can you handle it?"
"Yes. And what can I do for you?" asks 76.
"I need to do more penance," says 54.
"Okay, I can make sure of that," says 76. "And what about you, 04? Where do you fit into all this?"
"I'll make sure you and 54 meet each other back on earth and hold up your ends of the bargain. And then you'll become my parents."

On Looking Back After More Time Has Passed:
Lover of Leaving

my face: water flowing in a familiar way
eyelids like the undersides of leaves caught in currents
ceaseless movings on

my thoughts: a skeleton's worth of memories
dots behind my eyes like spray
foam on the ocean

not physical, but spiritual
soft, my skin against the rocks

not seeking, but sought after
thirsty, water comes to me

Timeline of the Stars and Love and Disaster Ends

100 trillion years from now
Stelliferous era ends.

When everything collapsed
something new formed
almost silently
because I found you
background noise
one strange sound
that never went away

10^{37} years from now
Degenerate era ends.

a signal unlike anything
under the stars
and you swallowed the stars
millions of them
over a lifetime.

10^{38} to 10^{100} years from now
Black hole era begins.

The way you pulled me in
I could not resist you
curved into darkness so dark
not even light could escape
this point of no return.

10^{100} years from now
Dark era begins.

I hope it gets easier
when I am gone.

QUATTRO NOVELLAS

The Ballad of Martin B. by Michael Mirolla
Mahler's Lament by Deborah Kirshner
Surrender by Peter Learn
Constance, Across by Richard Cumyn
In the Mind's Eye by Barbara Ponomareff
The Panic Button by Koom Kankesan
Shrinking Violets by Heidi Greco
Grace by Vanessa Smith
Break Me by Tom Reynolds
Retina Green by Reinhard Filter
Gaze by Keith Cadieux
Tobacco Wars by Paul Seesequasis
The Sea by Amela Marin
Real Gone by Jim Christy
A Gardener on the Moon by Carole Giangrande
Good Evening, Central Laundromat by Jason Heroux
Of All the Ways To Die by Brenda Niskala
The Cousin by John Calabro
Harbour View by Binnie Brennan
The Extraordinary Event of Pia H. by Nicola Vulpe
A Pleasant Vertigo by Egidio Coccimiglio
Wit in Love by Sky Gilbert
The Adventures of Micah Mushmelon by Michael Wex
Room Tone by Gale Zoë Garnett